# WALKING
## WITH
# MISS
# MILLIE

TAMARA BUNDY

# WALKING
## WITH
# MISS
# MILLIE

NANCY PAULSEN BOOKS

Nancy Paulsen Books
an imprint of Penguin Random House LLC
375 Hudson Street
New York, NY 10014

Library of Congress Cataloging-in-Publication Data
Names: Bundy, Tamara, author.
Title: Walking with Miss Millie / Tamara Bundy.
Description: New York, NY : Nancy Paulsen Books, [2017]
Summary: After moving with her mother and deaf brother to Grandma's
small Georgia town in the 1960s, Alice copes with feelings of isolation
by befriending the elderly black woman who lives next door.
Identifiers: LCCN 2016044878 | ISBN 9780399544569
Subjects: | CYAC: Family life—Georgia—Fiction. | Old age—Fiction. | Race
relations—Georgia—Fiction. | Deaf—Fiction. | People with disabilities—Fiction.
Moving, Household—Fiction. | Georgia—History—20th century—Fiction.
Classification: LCC PZ7.1.B8636 Wal 2017 | DDC [Fic]—dc23
LC record available at https://lccn.loc.gov/2016044878

Printed in the United States of America.
ISBN 9780399544569
3   5   7   9   10   8   6   4   2

Design by Eileen Savage.
Text set in Maxime Std.

*To Marshall, Jordan and Caleb*

*for reminding me that all that really matters is love*

# WALKING

## WITH

# MISS

# MILLIE

## chapter 1

The day we drove into Rainbow, Mama was pulling out all her tricks to distract us, trying to pretend we hadn't just left every one of our friends ten hours behind. "Oh, Alice! Look at my old hometown! See the trees lining the street? And the nice wide sidewalks? It's all so pretty!"

Out my window I saw a beat-up sign that once said, WELCOME TO RAINBOW, but now with most of the letters faded, it only read, COME RAIN, and that made more sense in this dried-up little town.

I remembered Daddy saying that the only good day in Rainbow, Georgia, is the day you leave. I used to laugh real hard when he said stuff like that. Then Daddy left

us—even though we weren't even living in Rainbow—
and I didn't think that joke was as funny anymore.

There's a lot that's not funny anymore.

Up till the last month of fourth grade, I was mostly
happy.

But then Mama called a family meeting. Family
meetings of the past had been for our cat needing to be
put down, us moving to a smaller house, and of course,
Daddy leaving.

So I knew better than to think that meeting was
going to be pleasant.

And I was right.

. . . . . .

"Alice." Mama's voice interrupted my thoughts. "Look at
that library over there. I used to spend so much time there.
You and Eddie will love it. Look how charming it is."

It was nothing more than an old brick house with
a wooden porch out front and a chalkboard sign
with the words CITY OF RAINBOW LIBRARY painted on it.
Underneath, someone had scribbled, *Make the summer of
'68 great—dive into a good book!*

Yeah, this was gonna be fun.

"And look, there. That's Emery Elementary, where
you both will start in the fall. Oh wait . . . don't tell Eddie

that. I'm not sure they can accept him—haven't talked to them yet. So don't tell Eddie about the school thing."

I wasn't telling Eddie anything. He fell asleep over an hour ago. I looked at him, snoring like he didn't have a worry in the world, still clutching the plate he always pretends is a steering wheel.

When Mama drives, Eddie does too. When she turns left, he turns the plate left. He's a real good backseat driver till he gets bored and wants a book or some toy. But still, he never lets go of that plate.

Back home, Eddie went to the Ohio School for the Deaf. Got in a big van to go to his school every day since he was three. Don't know why Mama thinks he will just be able to start going to a public school with me now that we live in this tiny town. Is he gonna walk through the door to a new school and just start hearing?

I was starting to worry about my mama's forgetfulness more than Grandma's.

When Grandma came to visit us last Easter, she got lost. She was driving to Columbus the same way she always did for every holiday. But this year she called from some diner way out in Pennsylvania. She shouldn't even have been in Pennsylvania! Even I knew that. I thought it was funny, but I remember Mama didn't laugh. She had this look on her face like a diner in Pennsylvania was the absolute worst place Grandma could ever end up. But Grandma eventually made it to our house just fine. Mama drove her back after Easter and then took the bus home. And I didn't think anything else about it.

Till Mama called the family meeting.

Mama told us Grandma's memory was getting worse and it wasn't a good idea for her to live by herself anymore.

I figured that meant Grandma would move in with us. I knew our house was small, but since Daddy left, Mama had the whole bed to herself, so I figured Grandma could sleep with her. At least until Daddy came back.

But Mama said no. Grandma's life was in Rainbow. She needed to stay where she knew people, where she'd spent most of her life. She needed to be in her home.

Not sure why Mama didn't understand that's what I needed, too.

## chapter 2

We turned onto Grandma's street.

I knew we were on her brick street because the road got so bumpy it woke up Eddie.

I looked at the other houses on the street. I'd been here to visit plenty of times before, but knowing we were staying longer this time made me look around like I was seeing it for the first time.

The paint on most everyone's shutters and front porches was the same shade of white. Or at least it used to be white. I could see it peeling on a lot of the houses. It looked like all it would take was one big wind to blow the chipped paint off and every house would be left stark naked.

Maybe that's why the houses all looked sad.

And Grandma's house looked the saddest of all.

As a matter of fact, I'd never realized it before, but her house was a big frowning face. I tipped my head to the side to see it better. The two upstairs windows sticking out of the flat roof were the wide-open eyes. The front door was a nose, and the shape of the peeling white rail of the wraparound porch, slanted on each side of the house, made a definite frown.

So there we were, plain as day, greeted by the entire house frowning at us. Guess nobody was happy about this move.

Except maybe Grandma.

She was out to greet us as soon as our car doors slammed.

When the car was moving, there was enough breeze to keep us from sweating. But now that we'd stopped, the heat took my breath away.

Eddie ran over to Grandma and gave her a big hug like always. Grandma can't sign to him, so she just talks extra-loud, like he'll hear that.

"Land's sake! Look at you!" And she did. Up and down like she was taking inventory of Eddie's arms and legs. "I think you've grown since Easter!" Of course Eddie did what he always does when people don't sign to him—he nods his head to make them feel better.

Mama went next to hug Grandma. But first Grandma held her at arm's length and announced, "It's always wonderful to see you all. But there is absolutely no need for you to uproot your entire lives to come here to watch over me like a teapot ready to boil. I'm a grown woman and I'm fine."

And she looked fine, too.

She was what Mama always describes as a perfect Southern lady . . . always dressed real nice. She only wears pants when she works in her garden. But any other time, she dresses like she's ready for church, as if all of a sudden she might get a call for an emergency church service and will be able to say, "No need to worry. I'm ready to go."

And right then, as I stared at her, thinking anybody who looked that nice couldn't be in need of being baby-sat, she finally turned to say hi to me.

"Alice! Look at you." She gave me a hug, squeezing me tighter than I wanted, and that's when I noticed she didn't smell as good as she usually did. She let out a high-pitched whistle before she shook her head and said, "You look more and more like your daddy every day!"

This was Grandma's favorite thing to tell me. Mama always says Grandma loves me, but it seems to me Grandma loves reminding me I take after my daddy in every way. And the way she says it, I can tell it's not a compliment.

By this time, Eddie had driven his plate in and out of Grandma's house. When he came back outside waving his hand in front of his nose, his face was all pinched up in a sign even Grandma could read, though she couldn't tell the next thing he signed was, "The house smells like the bathroom at the rest stop."

And he was right.

Grandma's house stunk and was a mess, too. There was a mountain of *Life* magazines in the corner, piled taller than Eddie. Two televisions were stacked one on top of the other in her living room. And what was that smell?

I saw Mama glancing around looking all worried, and I hoped beyond hope she was thinking we should head out and just leave.

But when she opened her mouth, instead of words telling us to get back in the car, her words were shaky like we were still on the bumpy road bopping up and down as she said: "Alice, you and Eddie need to stretch your legs and look around outside."

I know better than to backtalk Mama, so I did what she said.

As the back door swung shut behind us, Eddie took

off driving his plate around the backyard while I looked all around. On the right side of the yard was Grandma's garden, which was off-limits. Once last year, I kicked a ball into the middle of some flowers and you'd have thought the ball hit Grandma straight in the gut. I tried to make the flowers stand up again, I even tried propping them up with sticks 'cause I knew she'd be mad, but the more I walked around trying to help, the more I only messed the garden up. "Sometimes I wonder what on earth you're thinking!" she scolded me when she saw. "Just like your daddy," she added before walking back to the house.

I couldn't help noticing that the garden was drooping now, and looking less like the perfect blue-ribbon one she was known for.

On the left of Grandma's yard was a big old oak tree I liked to climb. But now the lowest branch was too high for me to reach. And the tire swing that used to hang from it was lying there all worthless on the ground beside the tree, like it, too, wasn't happy to be in this yard anymore.

Back in the far corner of the yard stood a rusty old shed where Grandma kept a lot of stuff for her garden. I wandered back there hoping to find something to stand on to hang the tire swing back up. Maybe if I fixed it, I'd have something to do in this town other than watch the flowers grow, or wilt in this case.

I entered the shed and found cobwebs hanging from every corner, draping down on rakes, and a wheelbarrow, and my mama's old bike. I grabbed a broom and swung it around to clear out the cobwebs so I could walk in.

That's when I noticed a box in the corner about the size of a shoe box and covered in faded gold paper that'd lost most of its shine. Still, one lone sparkle caught my eye enough to call me over. Squinting, I could make out my mama and daddy's names circled in a heart scribbled on the very top of the box.

This was a curious thing, for sure.

Bending down to pick up the box, I bumped into some stuff leaning against the old bike. The clanging thud of a rake falling echoed in the creepy silence of the shed just enough to make my heart pretty near jump out of my chest.

But what I saw on the bike was even scarier.

The biggest and hairiest spider I'd ever seen was sitting on that old bike. It didn't look too pleased that I'd bothered its quiet spot on my mama's bike either—and it might as well have been challenging me to a fight over who was the rightful owner of the bike.

I must've been staring down that big spider longer

than I thought 'cause the next thing I heard was a screechy voice yelling from somewhere in the backyard, "Hey! Anybody there? Anybody?"

I tiptoed out of the shed and looked in the direction of the voice. Before I could locate exactly where it was coming from, it started in again. "You there! Does this little man belong to you? Yes—you! Land's sake—is the whole family deaf?"

And that was my first almost-conversation with Miss Millie.

## chapter 3

I remember last summer Grandma talking about her neighbor Miss Millie. She'd been her neighbor for a while, but they weren't exactly friends. Grandma said it was 'cause Miss Millie just kept to herself. Grandma said the reason she kept to herself was 'cause she was a colored lady. I didn't get why when Grandma would say the word *colored*, she would kind of whisper it.

As I lifted up the bushes, finding the fence that divided the two yards, I finally saw Miss Millie.

She was tiny—Mama would say she probably weighed less than a hundred pounds soaking wet. She wore a man's button-down shirt and a long pair of pants, rolled up at the bottom. I couldn't imagine how she wasn't melting from the hot day. Her hair looked like a bunch of silver wires all joined together at the back in one heavy braid that went all the way down to her waist. Her face was a road map of lines.

I thought Grandma was old, but if she was old, Miss Millie was even older than Grandma. Heck, Miss Millie looked older than Moses.

Eddie didn't even take his eyes off her to look at me, and Miss Millie was looking back at him, kind of amused, like they shared a joke. Then she looked at me like she was determining what kind of person I was.

At last she spoke, extra-loud. "You deaf and dumb, too?"

I knew some people called a person who couldn't talk *dumb*, meaning he was mute and couldn't speak at all—but I didn't like that word. My brother, Eddie, wasn't dumb in any way.

But in all fairness, Miss Millie probably couldn't tell that my brother was smart since all he was doing, far as she could see, was standing like a statue in front of her with his mouth wide open like he was a bullfrog just waiting to catch flies.

"No, ma'am," I kind of mumbled as I watched Eddie snap out of whatever spell he was under when he saw me, and then start driving his plate all over Miss Millie's yard.

"Huh? You gonna have to speak up, girlie."

This time I yelled, "No, ma'am. My brother is deaf... but not dumb... He's not mute either."

"No need to yell," Miss Millie told me. "I'm old, not dead... yet." And she must have felt that was the funniest thing to say, because she started laughing, which turned immediately into a cough.

When it finally stopped, she turned to me and said, "So why's he doing that?"

But there was something in her voice this time that wasn't mean or anything, just curious.

"That's just what he does," I offered, realizing that explanation was clear as mud.

She continued to watch him as she shook her head. "Bless his heart. Can't hear a dang thing, huh?"

"Not a *dang* thing," I repeated, liking the sound of that word.

"Was it an accident?"

"No. Just born that way. He was in my mama's tummy when she visited a friend of hers and then found out the lady's kids had measles. After that, Eddie was born not hearing a dang thing."

Miss Millie and I both looked back at Eddie just driving his plate. I heard a bit of clicking coming from her mouth as she shook her head and sighed. "Don't seem fair."

"Guess not." I heard an angry barking and growling noise coming from the back door of Miss Millie's house then. Whatever was making that scary noise had to be huge and I didn't want to be around if it came out.

Miss Millie coughed a little more and cleared her throat. "So you must be Loretta's grandbabies?"

"Yes, ma'am." I was waving my arm to get Eddie's attention.

Finally, he looked at me, and I signed, "Let's go!"

Miss Millie let out a cackle. "Woo-hoo! Even I could tell what that means. Do you know all that fingerspellin' stuff?"

"Yes, ma'am," I told her, wanting to get away from the growling, which was getting louder and more worrisome. "Well . . . sorry to bother you. I'll tell Eddie not to come back anymore. He shouldn't have come over here. It's not right."

And with that, her whole tone changed and her face didn't look so friendly anymore.

"Well . . . sure. Sure he shouldn't be just traipsin'

about other people's private property. Hearing or not, he better learn not to trespass. I got a right to this property, you know."

I had no idea what I'd said to change her attitude.

All I knew was that I was ready to hightail it out of that yard—and hopefully out of Rainbow, too—for good.

## Chapter 4

When I got Eddie back to Grandma's yard, I talked him into going into the shed and getting that bike and box for me. He came out of the shed pushing the bike with the box resting on the seat, all the while grinning like it was the best bike in the world. He didn't seem to notice the rusted handlebars, the once-white wicker basket that was half on, half off, and the loose chain.

"You teach me," he signed, and pointed to the bike.

"No," I signed back, since I didn't know the first thing about teaching someone to ride a bike. "Daddy will teach you later."

Eddie shook his head, shaking loose a cobweb stuck in his hair. "Daddy gone. Daddy all the time gone."

I couldn't argue with that. This time, Daddy'd been gone six months. Time before that, it was three months. But each time, he came back. I knew he'd come back this time, too. Still, I couldn't explain all that to Eddie, so I just said, "We need to clean the bike up first and see if it can be fixed before anybody rides it." Eddie nodded like usual.

I picked up the little faded gold box from the bicycle seat. I could tell it was my mama's handwriting that once wrote her name and Daddy's inside the heart. It made *my* heart feel bad, wondering if Mama might still think she and Daddy belonged inside the same heart.

I sat down beside the shed, just looking at that dang box for the longest time like I expected it to talk to me or something. I couldn't bring myself to open it. Eddie sat down next to me. "What's in it?" he signed.

I shrugged in a sign everyone understood.

Eddie reached for the box and opened it. Inside there were envelopes—stacks and stacks of old, yellowed envelopes—all with my mama's name written in my daddy's handwriting.

A jumble of feelings raced inside me, trying to be felt at the same time.

I felt sneaky—like I shouldn't look at my mama's

letters from my daddy, knowing they weren't written for my eyes.

I felt happy to find something from my daddy when I was missing him so much.

I felt sad that yellowed old letters were all I had to make me happy about my daddy.

Eddie just peeked under the envelopes and shrugged in disappointment. He dropped the box and went back to seeing about fixing the bike.

"Help me fix," he signed.

I tucked the box back inside the shed, planning to return when Eddie wasn't around.

When we went inside Grandma's house to get some rags to clean the bike, the house smelled better, for sure, but I could tell Mama wasn't feeling any better about it. And other than the crazy, messed-up house, Grandma still seemed okay to me. I kept holding on to the hope that we'd be able to go back to Columbus, where I wouldn't have to hold yellowed letters to think of Daddy and he could teach Eddie to ride a bike and teach me everything else he hadn't taught me yet.

Sure, we gave the landlord notice and had a yard sale selling every single item that represented home to us. But I kept thinking we would head back north just as soon as Mama came to the rational conclusion that Grandma was fine.

. . . . . .

After cleaning that bike and finally fitting that chain back where it belonged, I tried to teach Eddie how to ride. Of course, as soon as Eddie realized he wasn't going to learn to ride it in a few minutes, he was bored with trying and went right back to his plate that he needed no lessons to drive.

While he drove his plate up and down the sidewalk in front of Grandma's house, I rode the old bike up and down the bumpy road, bouncing up and down, each time going a little farther than the last.

On my longest spin up the street, I went around the corner and all the way to Grandma's church—the only church in Rainbow. Up in Ohio we had all kinds of churches around us. We had a Catholic church, a Baptist church and even a Methodist church. But there's only one church in this little town.

I wasn't really looking for a kid my age to play with as I rode around, since it didn't matter to me at all— what with us not staying for long. But if I was looking, I would've seen only one kid out at all, and I couldn't tell if it was a boy kid or a girl kid. I could tell the hair was short and messy—making me think it was a boy—but there was something kinda girlish to make me wonder.

By the time I got back from that spin up the street, I realized I must've been gone for longer than I thought, 'cause in front of Grandma's house there were two kids— definitely boys, stopped on their own bikes. I could tell one of them was yelling at Eddie, who, of course, wasn't hearing any of it.

As I got close I heard the boy shout, "I asked you what ya was doin' with that plate! Y'all stupid or something? Answer me!"

When I heard those words, I pedaled my bike so fast the old brakes couldn't stop me soon enough. My bike ran smack into the bike of the boy not yelling, and I knocked both of us down. The yeller thought this was hysterical and burst out laughing. "Guess they're all stupid!" he said.

The boy I ran into was smaller than the one yelling. He got up, brushing himself off as I stood up, too. He reached out to my bike, and I yelled, "Don't touch it!" And then I turned to the yeller and yelled right back. "And you—don't say that about my brother. He's deaf but he's a lot smarter than you!"

By this time, Eddie was aware of something going on and he was standing next to us waving like he was happy to meet new friends. I signed to him, "Go up to the porch. These guys are not nice."

I picked up the old bike and began to walk away, but not before hearing the tall kid say, "Man, it's a family of freaks. Just what the neighborhood needs."

The other one said something, too, but I tuned them both out. My eyes stung with anger and the tears I was holding in. I stomped to the porch and dropped the bike so fast the just-fixed chain fell back off.

Eddie followed me and I saw in his eyes that he was waiting for me to explain. But I was so mad, I couldn't sign to him. I just shook my head and sat down on the porch swing.

But I've never been able to hide my feelings from Eddie. It's like because he can't hear, he can see things better.

"Why you mad?" he signed.

"I am mad," I answered with my hands, "because Rainbow is stupid! Moving is stupid! And everyone is stupid!"

As if the day wasn't bad enough, the sign for *stupid* is a fist up against your forehead, and when I signed it three times, being so stinkin' mad, I actually smacked myself in the head too hard. And it hurt.

My brother thought that was the funniest thing in the

world and started doing his own exaggerated *stupid* sign, pretending to fall over when he hit his head. "Stupid . . . stupid . . . stupid!"

I had to smile.

Eddie's movement made the swing sway back and forth, and I began to relax a bit. I took a deep breath and recognized the smell of Mama's chicken and dumplings coming from the house. I was just about to suggest to Eddie that we go inside to see if supper was ready when I heard the crunch of footsteps coming from the backyard.

It was Grandma walking toward the sidewalk in front of the house. She was in her nightgown.

Something told me she wasn't heading to a slumber party, and I just knew more bad news was about to pour down on us and Rainbow.

## chapter 5

"Grandma!" I hollered to get her attention since she looked kind of lost in spite of the fact she was only twenty steps from her house. "Grandma, what are you doing?"

"Hey, Joanie! Are you back?"

Since she called me my mama's name, I figured the sun, which was pretty bright, must be in her eyes. "It's me, Grandma. Alice. And Eddie's here. Why are you in your nightgown . . . and where are you going?"

Eddie of course saw Grandma, too, and I'm guessing he thought she was playing some sort of dress-up game, what with being outside in her nightgown and all. Still in a laughing mood from before, he started cracking up again.

But I could hear Grandma wasn't laughing.

Not at all.

"Oh, dear," she mumbled as I walked closer to her. By then, she was looking at the ground like she'd dropped something real important. "Oh, dear . . ." Her voice sounded all shaky and I feared she was about to burst into tears or something, so I ran inside to get Mama.

Mama helped Grandma back inside and took her to her room. She told Eddie and me to go ahead and eat, but even though my stomach was rumbling just a few minutes earlier, I kind of lost my appetite.

I popped a dumpling in my mouth and chewed it about fifty times, but it still felt like I was swallowing a biscuit whole.

That's when I heard the phone ring—but it wasn't the usual slow ringing like a phone from my house—it was more of a fast "ring-ring" sound like the phone tried to ring as usual, but instead just stuttered.

Since Grandma's only phone was in the living room and I knew she and Mama were busy—and 'cause I was hoping that phone call might be from someone like Daddy—I ran to the phone and picked it up.

But before I could say anything I heard a conversation already going on.

That's when I remembered Grandma had what's

called a party line, which sounds like it should be fun, but it's not really. It's just a phone line shared with her neighbors. Of course, as small as Rainbow is, I guess it's a wonder they don't all have to share just one phone for the whole town.

I listened to two ladies gossiping about the grocery store owner's daughter, Maddie, who was out late the weekend before with the son of the guy who works at the post office.

"Her daddy was madder than a wet hen when she come strollin' home way past when she oughta. Woo-wee! She might not see the light of day for a while. And who could blame her daddy? After her ma left the family in such disgrace. Well, you know the apple doesn't fall far from the tree . . ."

I had no idea who these ladies were talking about or even who these ladies were until I heard in the background the same growling monster noise I heard from the back fence all day and realized Miss Millie must be one of the ladies on the phone. She wasn't the one gossiping, but she was the one listening to the gossip when she wasn't saying, "Hush up! Hush up!" The barking, growling monster actually did hush up as Miss Millie offered up her own gossip. "Poor Clarence is almost completely blind now . . . can't see anything except—"

"Alice Ann!"

Mama's voice shocked me something fierce and made me drop the phone. I could hear the ladies on the phone saying something as I tried to put the receiver back. But somehow the phone suddenly seemed coated in butter and it took me three tries to hang up that dang phone, with it slipping all over the place.

Eddie didn't miss the little show I was putting on with the falling phone. He started laughing so hard, he spat out a dumpling. I thought if I tried to act sillier and make Eddie laugh, Mama would forget about me listening in on that conversation.

'Course Mama doesn't forget anything.

Ever.

"Young lady, were you eavesdropping on the party line?" It was definitely a question, but she didn't wait for an answer. "I can't believe it! Have I not taught you any better than that?"

Mama says stuff like that sometimes. Makes me feel lower than gunk on the bottom of a shoe.

"Sorry, Mama. I was bored . . . and the phone rang and . . . I really didn't hear anything. Just some gossip about the grocer's daughter and somebody's son." As soon as those words fell out of my mouth, I knew I was digging myself into a hole.

"Gossip? Now you're repeating gossip! You know we don't do that! Have you no morals?"

"No, Mama, it was only Miss Millie and some lady."

Mama's gasp made me realize that last bit of information wasn't helping my case. I needed to stop digging before I buried myself.

"So you knew who it was and you still continued to listen? Young lady, you need to march right over there and apologize to our neighbor Miss Millie."

"But Mama, I really didn't hear anything bad about her! She was just talking about a guy named Clarence who can't see anymore."

Mama stopped talking, which is usually worse for me than when she keeps talking. She took a deep breath. She looked older now than she had when we got to Rainbow just that morning.

Mama's a pretty lady. Real pretty. People always say so. She's got shiny, wavy brown hair that she usually wears pulled back in a ponytail. She only wears makeup on a special occasion, but everybody thinks Mama's pretty anyhow. 'Course most people always say how pretty my mama is right before they point out I don't look anything like her.

I look like my daddy.

Not that Daddy's not nice-looking, too . . . last I saw

him . . . blond hair and freckles, like me . . . but it's not the same. Now that I'm getting older I wish I looked more like my mama.

Mama exhaled and then announced, "Tomorrow, you will march over to Miss Millie's house and apologize for listening in on her private conversation. Then you will ask her if she needs help with anything." She turned to look at me like she wanted to make sure I was feeling the impact of her words.

I was.

"Maybe she needs something . . . or the gentleman who is going blind needs something. But you will say you are sorry, and offer to help. Do you understand?"

I swallowed the last bit of dumpling as I mumbled, "Yes, ma'am."

It's a wonder that food went down at all, what with my stomach doing flips just thinking about that growling dog I feared would swallow me faster than any old dumpling tomorrow morning.

## chapter 6

I woke up the next day hoping maybe Mama had forgotten about me eavesdropping on the phone and having a lesson to learn, but I might as well have hoped to sprout wings and fly back to Ohio, 'cause I knew better. Mama doesn't forget anything.

Right after I put the last breakfast glass in the dish drainer, Mama looked at me with one of those looks whose sole purpose is to remind me that she's the mama, and she said, "Might's well go take care of that little business now."

Grandma, who once again looked as right as rain, dressed in her nice clothes, wondered what was going on.

"Why is she going to Millie's?" she asked. "Be careful. I don't trust her."

"Mother! Why would you say that?" Mama whispered. "'Cause that's wrong if it's just because she's—"

"No. No," Grandma interrupted. "And maybe I am wrong, because Lord knows I get mixed up sometimes, but I swear sometimes I look out at my yard and I see her near my garden. What's she doing in my yard? Must be up to no good."

"Mother, I'm sure you're just . . . confused," Mama said. "I mean, she's lived behind you for years and she's always nice when I see her." She turned back to me. "Alice, get going."

And so with no reprieve, I walked slow . . . very, very slow . . . through Grandma's backyard, kind of like I was being sent to the principal's office at a school where the principal ate kids who were bad.

With each step toward that fence, I wished I was back in Ohio. Back home right now, I'd be getting ready for swimming lessons with my best friend, Linda.

We'd spend the day at the pool and hold hands and run and jump into the water. Then we'd see who could hold their breath the longest. Or sometimes we'd try to talk underwater to see if we could figure out what the other said.

And even if I had to keep an eye on Eddie, it'd be

okay since Eddie loved the sidewalks of the pool more than the pool itself. He could spend an entire afternoon driving his plate around the pool and the side shuffle-board courts, and nobody would bother him.

But I wasn't back home in Ohio and no wishing or walking slow could change that.

I peeked inside the still-open shed and saw the faded gold box sitting right where I left it. As much as I wanted to see what the letters said, I knew Mama would be mad enough to see I wasn't hopping the fence to talk to Miss Millie. If she noticed I was instead reading her letters, she'd really start to worry more about my morals. I pushed the box deeper into the shed to hide it just in case Mama came out there. Then, as slow as I could, I walked on.

Lifting up the tree branch that covered the fence separating Grandma's yard and Miss Millie's, I looked around.

On one side of the yard, I could see Miss Millie's garden and what was probably going to grow to be green beans and maybe some cucumbers. On the other side, there was a huge tree with an old picnic table underneath.

I was happy to not see any sign of the loud, ferocious dog I'd been hearing.

But just to be sure I wouldn't be hopping the fence

only to have my leg bit off, I whistled. One of the best things my daddy taught me was how to put my two pinkies in my mouth, curl up my tongue just right and let out a loud whistle. I was pretty dang proud of that whistle, too. People could hear it a block away.

Or just a house away, if they were a ferocious dog.

Right as soon as I whistled, I heard that horrible growling and barking coming from Miss Millie's house.

Now, I wasn't afraid of all dogs. Just big snarling dogs, like the one back in Ohio that used to scare me every day on my walk to school. Twice my size, he'd bark and growl and yank at his chain like he was threatening to get me. Every day I feared he'd pull that chain clear out of the ground and make good on that threat.

So now I was in a pickle and I had no idea what to do. What if Miss Millie opened the door and let the beast out because I'd started making him bark like crazy?

I sure didn't want to risk getting attacked by whatever was making that noise.

But if I stayed by the fence and she came out wondering who was whistling and upsetting her dog, she'd think I was rude for demanding an old lady come all the way to meet me at the fence just so I could apologize.

Worse than that, Mama would know I was rude.

So I took a deep breath, looked around one last time

(hoping it wasn't my honest-to-goodness last time I'd look somewhere) and I climbed that fence.

As I got closer and closer, the barking got crazier and crazier. I had to force my feet to keep moving . . . right foot . . . left foot . . . right foot . . . left . . .

When I was halfway to Miss Millie's back door, the beast managed to push open the screen and came bounding out in a brown blur.

I glanced back at the fence and knew I was too far away to make a run for it. Instead, I jumped up on top of the picnic table. I shut my eyes tight and on pure instinct, covered my face with my hands, maybe thinking if I didn't see how horrible the beast was before it used me as a chew toy, it wouldn't hurt as much.

I stood there ready to meet my Maker, hands covering my face for another minute before I realized the barking beast wasn't getting any closer.

I spread the fingers on my right hand far enough apart to allow me to get a look.

That's when I saw the beast . . . who wasn't such a beast after all.

Seems the only thing scary about that critter was his bark. The rest of him was just plain pathetic.

Not even coming up to my knees, this loud little guy was running in a circle as if he was angry at his own tail.

His short tan fur was no more than a blur to me, but I could tell he wasn't going to hurt me.

I let out a chuckle, which made him stop chasing his tail and stand still, snorting, like he was tracking down where the laugh at his expense came from.

I'd always heard dogs start looking like their owners after a while, and I was thinking that was true—that dog had about as many wrinkles as Miss Millie.

His face looked kind of smashed in though, like he was once chasing something and ran into it, face-first. He was mostly dirty white in color, but he had patches of tan, like God couldn't decide what color to make him. And right over his left eye was a splotch of tan placed so it looked exactly like an eye patch.

Just when I was sizing up this wrinkled, pirate-lookin' mutt, Miss Millie opened her back door and hollered, "Clarence! What you raisin' Cain for out here?" Then she squinted in my direction. "You again? Land's sake! Am I running a playground in my backyard?"

"Sorry . . . I . . . uh . . . I . . ." When I started to speak . . . or more correct, when I started to stutter, the dog . . . who I now realized was Clarence, started in with his barking, making it impossible for Miss Millie to hear me if I ever did get real words to come out of my mouth.

"Clarence! Come here. It's okay, boy. Come here . . .

come here." She walked over to the dog and picked him up and held him like a baby in her arms. I couldn't hear what she was saying to him, but it calmed him down.

I didn't know what to do, so I did nothing. I just stood there on top of the picnic table like I was auditioning to be a vase of flowers.

Then Miss Millie walked over to me. When she was close enough, I could hear a low grumble of a growl coming from Clarence, just like he was letting me know he wasn't quite the baby he appeared.

"So, Loretta's grandbaby, do ya have a name?"

"Yes, ma'am. I do."

She snorted at my answer. "Well, do I have to guess what it is, or might ya kindly tell me what it is—'specially if ya gonna be standin' on my table much longer."

"Oh, yeah, sorry . . . I was comin' to apologize . . . but the dog . . . I was scared . . . and . . . my name's Alice."

She looked at me like some people look at Eddie for driving his plate around. And then she started making a noise like she had a leak in her and air was coming out too fast. This air-leak sound soon gave way to an out-and-out belly laugh. A minute later, the belly laugh gave way to a coughing fit. Through the fit, Clarence just lay in her arms like she wasn't coughing but like she was singing him a lullaby.

Finally, I managed to say, "You okay?"

Miss Millie nodded while coughing like it was a speech she was used to giving, before finally stopping and continuing right on with our conversation. "Well, Alice-girl, my name's Millie, but ya probably knew that, didn't ya?"

"Yes, ma'am, Miss Millie, ma'am," I answered as polite as I could.

"And this here"—she nodded to the dog, almost asleep in her arms—"this here is my baby, Clarence. Can't see worth a lick, but he's still the best dog this side of the Mason-Dixon Line."

I had to stop myself from reaching out to pet the dog, who now resembled a pup cuddled in Miss Millie's arms. Looking at the two of them, it hit me even more how similar they were. Besides kind of wrinkly, both had a pretty loud bark. And so far, neither of those barks had turned into a bite.

But there was still time for that, I guess. Miss Millie looked away from her dog to take in the sight of me. "So, ya plannin' on standin' there all day, all week, all summer . . . ?"

"No, ma'am." I climbed off the table and took a deep breath. "I came over to apologize to you."

Even though that should've made Miss Millie smile,

it did the exact opposite. Instead, she tilted her head to one side and looked at me like she was trying to figure out what I was guilty of before I had a chance to confess. "Whatcha been doing to me, other than causin' all this racket, stirring up my dog and trespassing . . . twice in two days?"

"No, ma'am . . . I mean yes, ma'am . . . I'm sorry for those things, too. But what I'm apologizing for is last night . . ."

Her eyes squinted in concern. "Umm . . . hmmm . . . ?"

"Well, you see, the phone at my grandma's house rang and I went to answer it, and then I heard voices and realized it wasn't for Grandma. It was the party line." I said that last part like that would clear everything up. But Miss Millie just stood there not looking too clear, so I went on with my rambling. "I kept on listening even though I knew it was eavesdropping. So . . . I'm . . . sorry."

"Umm . . . hmmm?" she repeated, still looking at me sideways. But her mouth went from clamped up to curled up and I swear there was a hint of a smile as she asked, "Did ya hear anything . . . *good*?"

"No, ma'am. Just boring stuff about the grocer's daughter and her daddy being madder than a wet hen and apples not falling far from trees . . ."

"Well, don't that beat all," Miss Millie said. "Little pitchers got big ears . . . Heck! That wasn't much. Frankie calls me up ever so often justa hear her own self talkin'. She loves gossip more than fleas love dogs. No harm done."

I was relieved, but I knew Mama. And I had a feeling that if I came back and said Miss Millie said there was no harm done, she would find some harm in that and make me march right back and start the whole conversation over again. So I thought I'd try again. "My mama wants me to do something for you to make it right. Is there anything you need . . . um . . . any way I can help . . . or something?"

She smiled this time. "Well, that's mighty neighborly of your mama. But I think I have everything I need. I got this old dog right here." Clarence made a low growl just to say he knew she was talking about him.

I was thrilled. "Well, if you're sure," I said, and then just to seal the politeness, I added, never thinking it really meant anything, "I mean, just let me know if you think of anything."

And wouldn't you know?

Sure enough, she did.

chapter **7**

I'd almost made a clean getaway to the fence when I heard Miss Millie's voice from back where I left her and Clarence. "Hey . . . girl . . . Alice, was it?"

I turned around, wondering what I did this time.

"I maybe thought of something ya *could* do for me, for Clarence, I mean." Her voice was cracking a bit and I didn't want her to start coughing again by forcing her to talk too loud, so I walked back.

When I got close enough, she continued. "Poor Clarence here is pretty near blind. Ya saw him running in circles? That's 'cause he hears something and wants to find it, but can't see it in order to find it. Well, he can't even come out in the yard without hurting himself. But a dog who can't run in his backyard at least needs to walk. Maybe that's something a strong young 'un like you could help with?"

Now, I'd heard of guide dogs that help the blind, but did I have to be a guide girl for a blind dog? But I knew going home and telling Mama I helped Miss Millie by walking her blind dog would make things so much better than going home and saying there was nothing I could do.

"Sure?" I answered, knowing it sounded more like a question. "When do you want me to try to do that?"

"How 'bout right now?"

I couldn't think of one polite reason I could say no, so I agreed that now was as fine a time as any.

Miss Millie went over to that huge tree and grabbed a leather strap that was hanging on one limb. She put the tied loop at the end of the strap around Clarence, who wagged his tail like he was recognizing the sign for a walk. Miss Millie then handed the strap to me. "Here ya go. Maybe just up the street to Maple where the church is, and then back. That'd do him some good."

I pulled gentle on the leash to go.

But he didn't move.

Then I pulled a little bit less gentle on the leash.

But he still didn't move.

"Let's go, Clarence. Let's go for a walk to the church," I said, trying to sound all happy about the idea of the walk.

But Clarence wasn't having any of it. Not only did he not move forward, he actually moved backward.

Soon we had ourselves a regular tug-of-war going on. For a dog who couldn't see, he sure seemed to know it wasn't Miss Millie on the other end of that leash.

She even tried to coax him. "Come on, boy. Come on, Clarence."

But he wasn't gonna walk with me.

I can't pretend I wasn't a little bit happy right then. It wouldn't be considered my fault that the dang dog didn't want me to walk him. I was just waiting for Miss Millie to tell me I should stop trying.

But when Miss Millie finally spoke up, it wasn't to tell me to go on home. "Maybe if I walk with ya at first, he'll get to know ya better," she said. She took the leash from my hands and quick as a blink, Clarence was ready to walk.

But at the rate Miss Millie made us walk, summer would be over before we even made it to the church. For the second time in one day, I was counting my footsteps. Right foot . . . left foot . . . right foot . . . left.

I could hear Miss Millie struggling with her breathing. "Do you want to slow down?" I asked even though I had no idea how that would be possible.

"Nah, I'm okay," she kind of whispered. "This is what happens when you're ninety-two. The old ticker tick-tocks a little more slow these days." She wheezed when she said that, and I prepared for another laughing/coughing fit.

And this time when Miss Millie coughed, I saw a bike coming toward us. The overalls of the bike rider were the same ones I saw on the boy/girl in the yard yesterday. The closer the rider got to us, the more I could see that the person was actually a girl—probably a little younger than me. She smiled this big smile like she saw me walking with Miss Millie every day, and there was no doubt she was waving at us, not swatting flies. I looked at Miss Millie, who I assumed she was waving at, but Miss Millie was finishing up her coughing fit, so she could only nod and wave back to the bike rider as she passed us and then grew smaller riding down the street.

I was afraid to say anything or ask who the girl was what with it causing Miss Millie to talk and then cough again. I was planning on staying quiet as a mouse for the rest of the walk.

But Miss Millie was planning on something else. "So how long ya visitin' your grammy for?"

"I . . . uh, don't know . . . My mama says Grandma shouldn't live alone anymore, so she wants us to stay awhile to help her. But I don't think it'll be too long."

"Hmmm." Miss Millie seemed to know more than she was saying. "Guess time will tell, huh?"

"Yes, ma'am." I looked at Clarence, who was marching along with all the confidence in the world now that Miss Millie was guiding him.

I didn't want Miss Millie thinking I was stuck here forever, so I added, "Plus, my daddy, when he comes, he'll have something to say about it all. He hates Rainbow." I looked up at Miss Millie to see if she took offense at me not liking her hometown. She still looked straight ahead but I could tell she was listening by the way her head tilted toward me.

For some reason I needed to keep on talking about my family history. The words just kept coming and coming like they'd been waiting in a pot ready to boil and spill over. "Mama and he used to live here in Rainbow, even went to school here together, but Daddy said he needed to leave as soon as he had a chance. Said he couldn't breathe in a town so small. He needed a big city to be happy. Mama and Daddy got married right out of high school and moved to Savannah. That's where I was born. Mama says she wanted to call me Savannah, but Daddy said no. We lived there till I was five. That's when Eddie was born and we moved to Ohio."

I was rambling. And Miss Millie was just walking, breathing heavy and staring ahead into the empty space of the neighborhood. Just in case I confused her, I added, "Ohio is north of here."

Miss Millie, still walking slower 'n molasses, yet still breathing so heavy, stopped walking in order to get enough breath to say, "Land's sake, girl, I reckon I know where Ohio is." She whistled when she said the last word like the *s* got stuck between her teeth.

"Sorry. I just meant to tell you that even though I'm from these parts, and Mama says I still talk like I got some of the South deep in my blood, I'm just like my daddy—I don't belong here."

"Hmmm . . . ," she answered. "Is your daddy's family still in these parts?"

I shook my head, but that was kind of a fib. Truth was, I didn't know where Daddy's family was anymore. His daddy left him when he was little, and his mama, my other grandma, left Rainbow right after Daddy did.

There were some pictures of her holding me when I was a baby but I don't remember her any other way. But I didn't want to keep stammering on about my family's business to Miss Millie, so I just said, "No, they left. Like I'll do when Daddy comes to get us."

She stared straight ahead. "When might he be coming to fetch ya?"

"Oh . . ." I hated to admit it. "I don't know. I haven't seen him in a while."

"When's the last time ya saw your daddy, Alice-girl?" Her tone was kind, not at all accusing, but still, I felt ashamed to answer her the truth. "Right before Christmas . . ."

"Christmas? Well, shame. Shame on him for staying away from his family."

I don't like the fact Daddy has been gone that long. And I like it less when I hear Mama talking about him to her friends when she doesn't know I'm listening. But I like it least of all when a lady who has no idea who my daddy is says *shame on him*.

"It's not like that!" I objected. "My daddy's a good man. And he'll come back soon. I'd rather you not say any mean words about him, you hear?"

I couldn't tell whether it was the sunshine or the

anger making my cheeks burn so much. I shocked myself with my own words, knowing good and well Mama would have grounded me for the rest of the summer for being so rude.

I felt bad it all came out like that—bad and ashamed.

And I felt extra-ashamed when I saw we were at the corner of the street, right in front of the church and I saw a man I thought might be a new preacher since I didn't recognize him, but he looked like he belonged in front of the church. So now we can add yelling at old people to my list of sins for this week.

Miss Millie nodded to the man in question and hollered, "Morning, Reverend Hill."

"Good morning, Miss Millie. Might I expect you at service this Sunday morning?"

"You might. But then again, you might expect a lot of things that ain't likely to happen too soon." I didn't mean to let out a snort, but I had never heard anybody talk to a preacher man like that before.

He didn't seem to take offense at her words, just nodded, and looked at me as my face grew redder. Miss Millie pointed to me and told him, "This here young lady is just visitin'. Not stayin'. You can call her . . . *Savannah*."

The hint of a twinkle in her eyes let me know she

hadn't forgotten my name and was just pulling the preacher's leg. I nodded to him, figuring I might as well add lying to a preacher man to that long list of sins.

Miss Millie said goodbye to the preacher and we continued on our walk.

He hollered back to Miss Millie, "Door's always open, ma'am. Always open . . ." But by then we had turned Clarence around and were heading back to Miss Millie's house. She didn't say anything else about my outburst and I didn't want to talk about it again.

Still feeling ashamed, I changed the subject. "How long you had Clarence?"

Miss Millie smiled a smile that said she understood not to bring up my daddy again. Her wrinkles became more creased. "This guy here's been a part of my family since . . . I don't know . . . think it was 1960, something like eight years now. One day he was at my door and no one claimed him. So I guess ya could say he claimed me."

When she spoke about him, Clarence looked at her like he agreed that was the way it happened.

We walked in silence the rest of the way back to Miss Millie's. It seemed like we picked up a little bit of speed for the way home.

*A little.*

At one point, she quietly handed me the leash. But

even though Clarence wasn't looking, and can't even see for that matter, he stopped the minute the leash was in my hands and refused to move again.

Miss Millie took back the leash and said, "Maybe we could try tomorrow?"

This pretty much surprised me. I was certain I hadn't been the best of company. I mean, what with the yelling at her, and making her walk too fast and all. But maybe she really did want me to learn to walk Clarence by myself.

And maybe if I agreed to another day of walking I wouldn't feel guilty about yelling at her about my daddy. "Umm. Sure . . . Same time?"

"Good by me. I ain't exactly in demand around these parts. Unless, of course, President Johnson comes to town, then I might be busy. But he's in Washington, DC, I guess. That's also north of here."

And as she said that she winked at me and her whole wrinkly face smiled like it hadn't smiled in a long time and it just remembered how. I couldn't get mad at her even though I knew she was making a little fun of me.

I smiled back and turned to go. "See you tomorrow, then."

"Wait, Alice-girl. Let me give you something."

By now we were in her backyard and she let Clarence

off his leash and he wasn't growling at me for once. Miss Millie went over to her picnic table and I saw her pick something up off the table for me.

She extended her hand and took ahold of mine. Her hand was rough and worn with age and work. When she opened her hand, something shiny and little landed in my palm. I sensed the coolness of its smooth surface before I saw what it was.

It was a blue marble.

What on earth was I supposed to do with a marble? But I remembered my manners and managed to say, "Thanks. It's real pretty. See you tomorrow."

When I got back to Grandma's house, Mama was honest-to-goodness happy to hear about the walk and all. And when I showed her the blue marble, she looked at it and got all misty eyed, like it was the best treasure in the world.

I asked, "Mama, why'd she give me a marble?"

And Mama hugged me as she answered, "I don't know—maybe we all just need somebody to share things with."

That sure didn't help. "So . . . Miss Millie just wanted to share a marble with me?"

Mama smiled and shook her head. "Something tells me she's sharing more than that."

I still didn't understand why Mama was so happy with that marble. "Do you want it?" I asked, not really wanting to give it away, but seeing how happy it made her.

She hugged me again. "That marble's yours, Alice Ann. And maybe you don't realize it yet—but it's like a ticket to heaven."

I took the marble back, still not sure what she was talking about.

Guess mamas just say stuff like that sometimes.

## chapter 8

The next day, I had my breakfast, but skipped the washing-dishes part—no need to try to butter up Mama when she was in the middle of teaching me a lesson.

But this time, before I hopped that fence to Miss Millie's, I made a pit stop at the shed. I picked up the box and sat behind the shed—out of view of the window just in case Mama was watching.

Opening the box once again, I took out the top letter. *Joanie* was written on the front, and on the back was written *SWAK*—which I remembered Mama saying meant *Sealed with a Kiss.*

For a few minutes I tossed around in my mind the

idea that it wasn't stealing somebody's letters if they were already opened and left out in an old box for years. I mean, if these old things meant something to Mama, wouldn't they be in a safe place today?

And of course, if Daddy meant something to Mama, wouldn't he be here today, too?

Mad at that last thought, I took out the first letter.

It was a poem.

*The sun's golden rays*
*danced in your hair.*
*You looked in my eyes*
*and asked if I care.*
*How could I explain*
*my feelings so true*
*as I sat there that day*
*by the wishing well with you?*

That was so sweet, but it made me shake my head. I didn't even know Daddy liked poems or that he could write 'em. When Daddy called, maybe I could ask him about it.

I stuffed the letter back in the box and the box back in the shed and I walked toward Miss Millie's.

I hopped over the fence and waited to hear if there was any sign of Clarence. I wasn't afraid of him like the day before, but still, I didn't want to set him off on a barking fit.

I didn't hear any barking, but I did hear something else coming from the house. And this sound sounded good.

Music.

I went to knock on the screen door, but I stopped for a moment to listen. It was a scratchy recording of "Over the Rainbow" from the movie *The Wizard of Oz*, where Dorothy is real sad she's stuck in Kansas. I grinned thinking about this Thanksgiving, when I'd get to watch it again on TV, like we did every year. But what made me smile even more than that was the other sound I heard. Along with the scratchy record, I heard Miss Millie.

*"Somewhere over the rainbow, skies are blue. . ."*

When the song ended, Miss Millie held out the last word like she was singing on a stage. While her voice was a little shaky, it was still nice to listen to.

Sometime from when I started listening to the music to now, I must have opened the door to hear better, so when Miss Millie saw me, I was just standing there with her door half open.

"Land's sake, girl," Miss Millie scolded. "You born in a barn? Shut that door before I get more flies in here than a pigsty."

She was trying to sound mean again, but I didn't believe her this time.

Clarence, on the other hand, did sound mean. As soon as he realized I was standing in his house, he began his beastly barking and growling.

And there was nothing pretty about it.

"Hush now, Clarence! Hush!"

This time Clarence actually obeyed and came over, sniffing me like he was sizing me up.

"See there, he's makin' a friend." Miss Millie kind of laughed. "'Course I'm surprised he recognized ya at all, what with ya not standin' on my table." She laughed and coughed a bit. "Maybe he'd let ya walk him today by yourself."

But again, Clarence had other ideas.

After a few minutes of the same tug-of-war as the day before, Miss Millie offered to go along, too, one more time.

It was still hot. *Real hot.* I didn't think I'd ever get used to the Georgia heat and was glad I wasn't gonna have to stay down here for long.

We walked slower than molasses again, but Miss Millie wasn't breathing quite as hard as the day before. As a matter of fact, she was whistling "Over the Rainbow." Walking and whistling, just like she was perfectly capable of walking her own dog.

She was holding the leash and I was just walking slow beside her, feeling pretty useless, and sort of mad that I even had to be there.

All of a sudden, Miss Millie stopped and turned to me. I started worrying I had said that last part out loud and hurt her feelings. She just squinted her eyes so much they disappeared as she looked at me. "Alice-girl, I owe you an apology."

I didn't know what to say, so I just stood there looking at her.

"Yesterday I butted into your family business when it was no business of mine. I'm sorry for what I said about your daddy. I'm sure he's a fine man."

Didn't that beat all? I sure wasn't used to adults apologizing for having opinions. So I stammered a bit: "That's—that's—okay. I'm sure if you knew Daddy— When he comes, maybe you can meet him . . ."

Miss Millie looked sad as she answered, "Hmmm . . ." And again, I felt she knew more than she was saying.

For some reason, I needed her to like my daddy. "He writes real nice poems, you know? Real nice—about wishing wells and things."

She smiled at that. Then she added, "That's nice. And that's a good idea. I'll meet him when he comes to fetch ya."

We continued to walk to that corner by the church and this time the preacher wasn't outside when we got there. I remembered his conversation with Miss Millie the day before and I was curious. "Why don't you like church?" I asked her.

Miss Millie snorted and it sounded a little like Clarence. "Now, who says I don't like church?"

"I thought you said that. Yesterday, you said you weren't going to church."

"Never said I *don't like* church—plenty of things to like about church. But what I don't take a shining to are people who act one way all week, but come Sunday, they dress up, go to church and then go right back to doing mean, un-Christian-like stuff the rest of the week. I just got tired of people being phony."

She continued to walk real slow. I could see her looking up into the clouds like they were reminding her what to say. "We used to have a separate Negro church in the town next to Rainbow. It was a nice place. But when the last preacher left, no one was sent to take his place. The new preacher man at this church here on the corner keeps invitin' me and I might go every now and then, but I just don't make it often anymore."

"You had separate churches for black people and white people?"

"Alice-girl, this here's the South. Up till a few years ago there was nothin' but separate things for us. There were separate places for sittin' on a bus, drinkin' from a fountain, or usin'"—she paused for a minute looking for her next word—"the *facilities.*"

Now, I was getting ready to go into fifth grade this year, so I knew about how unfair things were for black folks—'specially in the South. And I knew that just a couple of months ago Reverend King was assassinated. But I guess I never really thought a whole lot about it because at my school in Ohio we only had one water fountain and a boys' bathroom and girls' bathroom for everybody. It didn't make sense, Miss Millie being told where she could and could not go like that.

"Things still like that today?"

"Well, Alice-girl," Miss Millie said, "I don't go many places these days. I stay right here and mind my own business—usually keeping to myself till somebody hops my fence or listens in on my conversations . . ." Again she winked at me. "But child, there's still lots of places in the South that make people like me feel like we don't belong. Laws might change—but some people never do."

"That must make you mad," I said.

Miss Millie kind of laughed. "It used to make me mad. But I learned a long time ago things are what they are. My brother tried to change things though . . . and it didn't do him one lick of good."

"You had a brother?" For some reason, picturing Miss Millie with a brother made me picture her as a young girl. But even thinking of her as a young girl, I found myself picturing her with wrinkles.

"I did. I had me a baby brother. Few years younger than me. He was a good man."

I saw Miss Millie's wrinkles crease even more like her face pinched up just thinking about it. I had to know. "What happened to your brother?"

She stopped and looked at me from head to toe like she was trying to figure out something about me, and I guess she was. "How old are ya, Alice-girl?"

I stood up straighter like that would make a difference. "Almost eleven," I announced.

Miss Millie turned to walk again as she nodded her head up and down real slow. "Reckon almost eleven is pretty near old enough."

She continued to walk and I continued to get more and more curious about what I was pretty near old enough for, until she finally started her story. "I was born and raised in Atlanta. Little west of here." She smiled. "But I picked a tough time to come into the world."

Now I was remembering my history books. "Were you ever a slave?"

Miss Millie looked shocked. "Land's sake, Alice-girl—how old do ya think I am? I'm not over a hundred . . . yet!" She laughed and coughed a bit before continuing. "My mama was born a slave—but slavery was ended when she was a young woman. 'Course then she was free—but with no education, no job and by then no parents. Hard times for my sweet mama . . ."

Miss Millie's voice trailed off as we reached her house. She bent down to take off Clarence's leash, but even with it off, he stood by her feet, like he wanted to hear this story, too.

Miss Millie waved her hand in front of her face like a fan. "How'd I get off on this tangent about my life history? Woo-wee! Must be borin' ya to tears. I'm gonna sit a spell over there by the picnic table. You can go ahead and go if ya want." She walked to the table and took a long time to sit down, like she was lowering herself one bone at a time.

I followed right behind Clarence, who was following right behind her, and seated myself across from her at the table. "So can you please tell me what happened to your mama . . . and your brother?"

She took a deep breath like the oxygen she was breathing in might help trigger her memory to come out better. But something told me she could live to be a hundred and fifty and never would be able to forget what she was saying. "By the time Mama met Daddy, things were tough all over. They were stuck in the South but the South wasn't too happy to have 'em stuck here. Daddy picked up jobs workin' on plantations tryin' to get the money to head North. Soon I joined the family and when I turned eight, my brother come along."

She looked at Clarence and then back at me. "My brother—name was James—well, James was smart. He even got himself into college. Yessiree, he was smart, but angry. He saw the differences for us folks in education, jobs—everything. Back then, if a white person didn't like the way a black person looked at him, he could shoot him and no questions asked."

I gasped when those words hit me.

Miss Millie looked back at me and nodded. "Hard to believe, isn't it? James thought so, too. The year was 1906 when him and his friends decided to take a stand and fight for justice. The Atlanta Riot is what they called it. But I just call it sad."

She breathed deep. "Paper said over twenty-five black men were killed during that time. But those of us closer know it was more like a hundred. But however you count it, my one and only brother was killed."

As she stated this statistic, she bent down to pick up Clarence like she needed a hug or something.

I felt like giving her a hug, too, but just as I started to scoot closer to Miss Millie, I saw Eddie hopping the fence.

For once, he didn't have his plate. From where he stood, he signed, "Mama want you come home and help with Grandma. Now."

Right then I didn't want to go. I had just dug deep in Miss Millie's memory and stirred up something painful. To up and leave while the pain I forced to leak out was still so raw seemed downright wrong.

I signed back to Eddie as I said out loud, "Tell Mama

I can help with Grandma in a few minutes" but he shook his head as his pointer fingers ran down his cheeks, telling me my mama was crying.

I couldn't be any more torn two ways if he'd grabbed me on one side and Miss Millie and Clarence grabbed the other and both started pulling as hard as they could. I looked back at Miss Millie, who smiled like she understood sign language all of a sudden.

"Guess ya gotta go?" She reached into her shirt pocket and pulled out what I thought was another marble, but when she stretched her hand across the picnic table to put it in my hand, I saw it was a rock. "Here ya go, Alice-girl. Thanks for the walk."

The rock was black and shiny with something sparkling through the middle of it. Holding it in my hand, studying it like it just appeared out of nowhere, I probably looked like I was trying to figure where it came from, and Miss Millie must have guessed my question before it was asked. "That . . . and the marble from yesterday. They both belonged to James."

"It's real pretty," I said. "Looks like a diamond river runs through it."

She nodded. "James said that that there rock reminded him that no matter how dark the world seemed at times, there was still beauty to be found in it." She smiled deeper. "Yessiree, he was a smart man, my brother."

I think I did a better job that day of thanking her than I did the day before.

And I didn't even have to ask about tomorrow's walk.

I just knew.

## Chapter 9

When I got close to Grandma's house, I heard a man's muffled voice coming from inside and for one minute, I thought it was Daddy. I swung open the back door with a thud and almost ran smack-dab into the doctor.

He was an older man with white hair and whiskers and he chuckled at me coming to such a quick stop.

Mama seemed to know him a lot better than she ever knew our doctor in Columbus.

"Now, Joanie, ya know your mama's gonna have good days and bad days. There's no way of knowin' how fast or slow her memory might decline." The doctor spoke with a thick Southern accent. "And I am happy to oblige her with a house call, but there is really nothin' to do at this point 'cept keep her safe. And of course, pray."

Mama wiped her eyes with the back of her hand, making her look almost like a little girl and not like a real mama. "Thanks, Doc. I can always count on you."

He smiled, giving her a hug. "Well, since I brought ya into this world, the least I can do is help ya get through it, don't ya think?"

Mama grinned at him and then looked at me. "Alice, you remember Dr. Reilly?"

He bent down to be eye level with me. "Hello, Alice. You have definitely grown since the last time I saw ya. You certainly are a lovely young lady. Must take after your mama."

I figured the doctor's eyes were getting old. Nobody says I take after Mama. But when he said that, I smiled. And I might have even blushed. He held his hat in his hand by his chest when he bent down, but moved it toward his head, like he was tipping it to me when he stood back up.

"Now, if'n ya lovely ladies will excuse me, I'll go have a look at the patient."

As he left I saw Eddie standing by the back door, watching. Usually, he has lots of questions when people aren't signing around him. Since he just stood there watching, I knew he was worried.

Mama knew it, too. "It's okay," she signed. "Sorry to worry you. Grandma is okay now."

Eddie nodded and went back outside, but something told me he didn't believe Mama's words any more than I did.

"What happened to Grandma?"

Mama looked toward Grandma's room and then back toward me. She answered in a voice just barely above a whisper. "She woke up confused today. Didn't know where Daddy—your grandpa—was. When I reminded her he died five years ago, she took the news hard, like she was learning it for the first time." Mama's voice choked. She stared at Grandma's bedroom door like she was lost for a moment. Then she nodded her head. "It's good we're here, Alice. It's so good we're here." She walked over to the window to watch Eddie in the backyard.

When Mama first told us we were moving to Georgia at that family meeting back in Columbus, I told her right away I didn't want to move. No, I told her I wasn't gonna move.

Ever.

But just when I was working on my best arguments to convince Mama why we shouldn't move, she took my hand in hers like she was really holding on to me and said in a voice I could barely hear, "It's the right thing to do. It'll be okay. I promise." Then she lowered her head to rest on our hands and when she lifted her head, I saw tears in her eyes and that's when I knew we were moving to Rainbow.

There are a few things I just can't handle. Broccoli and poison ivy, for sure. But worst of all is my mama crying. Up till last year, I was okay with Mama crying—I mean, it's not like I liked it or anything, but it didn't hurt me on the inside. But lately, when Mama's eyes get all misty, my own eyes decide they have to get misty, too. And I hate that.

And now, standing in Grandma's kitchen, with Mama about to cry, I still didn't want to be in Rainbow, but I knew we were probably stuck here.

Even more than that, I knew I didn't want my mama to cry.

I walked over to her and hugged her around the waist. She bent down and kissed the top of my head. "What would I do without you, Alice Ann?"

Mama sniffed a few times and then seemed to remember where I'd been. "How'd your walk with the dog go today? Did he let you walk him?"

"Nah. He only likes Miss Millie walking him. So we all walked together again today."

"How was that?"

My conversation with Miss Millie came back to me and I said to Mama, "Did you know that Miss Millie had a mother who was a slave and a brother who was killed for protesting about how bad black people were treated?"

Mama tilted her head to look at me. "Well! It sounds like you two are doing a lot more than walking a dog. Miss Millie has sure been through a lot."

"She has . . . ," I added like I was an expert on her by now. "She gave me this today." I reached in my pocket and showed Mama the rock.

"This was her brother's," I said. "Doesn't it look like there are diamonds running through it?"

Mama smiled. Real big. "It's beautiful," she said, and then she asked, "Do you know when her brother was killed?"

I thought back to our conversation. "It was 1906." I was proud of myself for remembering.

Mama nodded. "So Miss Millie thought this rock was worth holding on to for more than sixty years, but she gave it to you today. That means this rock—and *you*—must be pretty special."

Not sure if it was the heat, the emotion or the pride I was feeling right then, but my cheeks burned and my eyes stung as I squeezed that rock tighter.

Chapter **10**

When I got to Miss Millie's house the next day, she was sitting exactly where I left her at her picnic table and I started to worry that maybe she was getting Grandma's forgetful disease. But then I saw she had on different clothes from the day before. She still wore a man's button-down shirt, but it was a different color. Miss Millie's hair looked newly braided, too.

Clarence barked and snorted, but only for a few seconds. Soon he was sniffing me again, and he must have recognized my smell because he stopped on his own without Miss Millie needing to say *Hush* or anything. I wanted to reach out and pet him, but stopped myself. Even though I wasn't scared of him anymore, I wasn't yet sure how he felt about me.

"Everything okay over at your grammy's house?" Miss Millie asked.

"I guess." I tried to sound happy, but I think she could hear the sad sticking to my voice like my hair was already sticking to my neck.

The day before, I made it through talking to Mama about Grandma thinking Grandpa had just died without me crying. I made it through hearing the doctor say there's not a dang thing he can do for Grandma without me crying. And hardest of all—I even made it through hearing Mama cry last night when she thought I was asleep, without me crying.

So when Miss Millie asked me if Grandma was okay, imagine how surprised I was to find my eyes getting all misty. And before you know it, I was telling her everything and those dang tears were flowing like a fountain.

Miss Millie sat there nodding her head as she reached in her shirt pocket and fished around for a hankie she pulled out for me so I wouldn't flood her backyard. Every now and then she would say, "Poor baby," and I wasn't sure if she was talking about Grandma, Mama or me, but it didn't matter, 'cause it made me feel better.

I stared at the hankie she gave me, noticing the initials *MM* and real pretty lace all around. It struck me as something so ladylike for someone wearing a man's shirt to have.

"Can you keep a secret, Alice-girl?" Miss Millie asked after my tears decided to stop.

I nodded my head quick to tell her I could.

Miss Millie looked at the ground like she was embarrassed about something. "I . . . I . . . kind of figured your grammy was having a problem when her garden was never watered and the plants started dyin'. She's always so proud of that there garden and I knew she wouldn't let it die on purpose. So I kind of been waterin' it from time to time."

Right then and there you could have knocked me over with a feather. 'Cause all of a sudden I remembered Grandma saying what she said about Miss Millie being in her yard and thinking she was up to no good, when all this time she *was* up to good, keeping her garden from withering up and dying. Didn't that beat all? I sat there with my mouth open for all to see, like I was waiting for the words to fall out by themselves.

Miss Millie sat there also waiting for those words to fall out, with this look on her face that reminded me of what my face must look like when I'm waiting on Mama to scold me for something.

Finally, my words decided to fall.

"You mean all this time, you've been watering her garden?"

"I'm sorry . . ." Miss Millie looked hurt and a little embarrassed. "I probably shouldn't a gone over there, but—"

"That's the nicest thing I ever heard," I interrupted. "It's the nicest thing in the world!"

Miss Millie smiled then. It started in her eyes and found its way to her wrinkled mouth. But just when the rest of her face was showing an out-and-out smile, she turned it off like she had an on/off happiness switch inside her. I could tell, though, she was only pretending to be fed up with the whole conversation because her eyes were still smiling.

"Oh, fiddlesticks! Stop carryin' on with such non-sense. No need to nominate me for the Nobel Peace Prize 'cause I kept your grammy's tulips alive. And no need to tell her what I done." She turned away from me, but not before I figured out she was blushing. Yep. I didn't think it was possible, but Miss Millie was honest-to-goodness blushing.

I just stood there shaking my head, taking it all in till Miss Millie picked up the leash and put it around Clarence. "This here dog is wonderin' if we'll stop blab-berin' long enough to take him on a walk. Ready?"

And from that moment on we didn't even try to have me walk Clarence by myself. It was always kind of understood that I was walking Miss Millie . . . who was walking Clarence.

. . . . . .

Miss Millie suggested we change our walk a bit that day and all of a sudden we were walking by the cemetery.

I mean no disrespect to the dead when I say that I don't like cemeteries. It's just a fact.

I remember going to Rainbow's cemetery when Grandpa died. 'Course I wasn't supposed to go to the funeral at all. Mama got a sitter for me and Eddie, who was just a baby. But when the sitter was putting Eddie down for a nap, I decided to go find Mama. Walked straight to the cemetery and right through the big iron gate. But I must've turned right when I was supposed to turn left or something 'cause I didn't find Mama or anyone for a long while—just kept running into tombstones, all scared and alone, until a nice old man finally heard me crying and helped me find everyone.

Last summer, Mama took Eddie and me to "pay our respects" to Grandpa. Eddie drove his plate along the paths of the cemetery. I just held tight to Mama's hand.

I had no idea if Miss Millie was just walking by the

cemetery for a change of pace, or if she planned to pay her respects to any of her dearly departed. Then I had to wonder if she even had any dearly departed.

"Is your brother here?" I asked.

"In Rainbow?" Miss Millie's voice squeaked a bit. "Alice-girl, I told ya he was killed in the Atlanta riots some sixty years ago."

"I know." I didn't want to spell this out, but I had to. "I mean is he *here*?"

"No, child. James is buried in Atlanta."

As we entered the cemetery I noticed that the old iron gate was rusty, like it had seen better days. But then, I guess everyone in the cemetery had seen better days, too.

I was hoping we'd turn around and head home, since James was in Atlanta, but Miss Millie walked on into the cemetery, past the pretty headstones with fancy-lettered names and descriptions of the deceased such as *Beloved* and *Devoted*. We walked past the nice fake flowers people put on graves since nothing could stay blooming in the Georgia heat. We had walked past what seemed to me to be the entire cemetery, when Miss Millie finally stopped our walking. She stood next to a white wooden cross that came up out of the ground to about my knees, and smiled.

I moved to see what she was looking at. When I got closer, I could read what was left of a peeling name on the old white cross: *Clayton Miller, loving husband and father. 1874–1958.*

I looked again at Miss Millie, who now looked like she was trying to decide if she was going to continue smiling or start crying.

"Did you know Mr. Clayton Miller?" I asked.

"I reckon I do know Mr. Clayton Miller, God rest his soul, seein' as how I'm Mrs. Clayton Miller."

"So that would mean he was . . . you were . . . Were you *married*?"

"That's how it works, girlie!" And as she tried to laugh at her joke, she started coughing that cough again that began down in the middle of her and bubbled out. Clarence and I knew to wait for her to be finished with her coughing fit. While she was wheezing away, I turned back to that cross, like it was going to all make sense this time. There it was, written about Clayton Miller, loving husband and father.

*And father?*

Like when Miss Millie told me about being little with her brother, there was no way I could conjure up a picture that made her look like anything other than the old lady with all the wrinkles who was standing in front of me now. I suppose that's why at that moment my brain was refusing to take in this latest detail about her life.

If my brain had windows to let stuff in, I guess when I came to Rainbow all my windows were closed, but now Miss Millie and Mama were giving me more stuff every day to let in, demanding those windows open up. Maybe that's what being almost eleven feels like.

When Miss Millie finished her coughing routine, I had to ask. "So if you were married and he was a loving father, you must be a loving mother, right?"

"I'd sure like to think I was a loving mother," Miss Millie told me, her eyes glistening. "Didn't have him long enough, though."

I looked around at the other grave markers. "Is he here, too, I mean, in the cemetery?"

She smiled a sad smile as her eyes filled with more tears. "Nah. My boy died long before we moved to Rainbow. God rest his soul. But that's a story for another day. I just hadn't visited Clayton for a while and thought it'd be nice and pleasant to stop by."

Miss Millie held her hand out to the cross and touched it, but not like it was holding her up. But, seeing her smile, I figured maybe it was kind of giving her strength. I watched as her lips moved but I could tell the words weren't for me, so I was real proud of myself for not eavesdropping again and just staying quiet for a few minutes.

Since Clarence was being polite, too—I noticed he wasn't doing his business in the cemetery—I bent over to pet him for the first time. And would you believe that dog let me? It was like we had a little moment between us, of both of us staying out of the way. For Miss Millie.

His bottom tooth stuck out from under his top teeth and it looked like he was making a face at me on purpose to make me laugh. I patted his head and before I could say *Good boy!*, he was laying down on the dirty ground, showing me his belly. Next thing I knew, I was plain-as-day rubbing his belly and he was plain-as-day liking it.

Soon enough, Miss Millie was done with her conversation and she turned back to me and Clarence. "Thanks for bringing me today." She said that like I was the one who brought her here. It made me feel—I don't know—it made my heart kind of swell.

She and Clarence began to walk away as I stole one last look at Mr. Clayton Miller's grave marker. That's when it hit me!

"So if you were married to Clayton Miller, that would make you—"

"Go ahead and say it." I swear she was smiling so hard she was almost busting her face.

"Millie Miller!" I snorted a snort that would have mortified Mama.

Miss Millie didn't seem to mind my unladylike laughter. She seemed to like it. "Yep. That's me. Heard all the jokes. Guess it makes it easier to remember, don't ya think?"

I giggled as we walked back toward the cemetery's gate, which seemed even farther away on the way out. I looked again at the big grave markers at the front of the cemetery and thought of the peeling little cross of Miss Millie's husband way in the back.

"Was the cemetery like the churches?"

"Huh?" Miss Millie had to huff a bit to catch her breath. "What ya mean?"

"I mean, were there separate cemeteries for black people and white people?"

She smiled. "Ah, so ya noticed there was a little difference in the graves, huh? Well, ten years ago, I had to go and get permission to bury my husband in this here cemetery. They weren't exactly happy about it. But I didn't give up and they finally agreed to let me bury him here if I took that back space away from everybody. Since then, other colored folks joined Clayton, and today it's a little more mixed up."

Mixed up seemed to me to be a good description of that whole separation thing.

When we got back we were both covered in sweat. It was stinkin' hot, even in the shade. The visit to the cemetery took longer than our usual walks, and I knew I'd better be getting back to Grandma's, so there was no sitting for a spell.

But before I left, Miss Millie reached into her shirt pocket again and pulled out something. As she put it in my hand, I saw it was an old picture—kind of cracked-looking, but I could still see who was in it. It was a young couple smiling for the camera. The woman had a familiar long braid down her back, but the hair wasn't at all wiry and gray; it was coal black and shiny. And she wasn't at all wrinkly—she was young and pretty. And on her lap was a little guy, maybe two or three years old, and he was smiling up at his mama like she was the best lady on earth.

"Was this your family?"

She nodded real slow like this time she had to wait for the words to fall out of *her* mouth. "It was my family . . . It *is* my family."

In the short time I'd known and walked with Miss

Millie, I hadn't seen her sentimental and she wasn't going to get too mushy now. She leaned toward Clarence, who was also looking up at her like she was still the best lady on earth, and said, "This here little fellow is my family now."

I looked again at the picture before handing it back to Miss Millie. She shook her head. "You keep it."

"But it's your family. You need it."

She shook her head once more. "I've got that picture and hundreds like it right here . . ." She pointed to her heart. "That's all I need." She put her hand on top of the picture in my hand. "Knowing someone else can remember my family, too, means we live on."

I still had no idea what I was supposed to do with James's marble and rock or now this old picture.

But I was sure that when Miss Millie gave you a present like that, you had to take it.

So I did.

## chapter 11

I never know what Eddie is going to find fascinating, besides of course that dinner plate that keeps him occupied pretty near all the time.

But when I hopped the fence, he noticed right away I was carrying something. Like I said, he's good at noticing things. Mama says when God takes away one sense, He gives extra helpings of the others, and that's sure true about Eddie 'cause he doesn't miss a thing.

So I showed him the picture and he just stared and stared at it, like his heart was trying to memorize it, too. Finally, he turned to me, making an invisible circle around his lips, which is the sign for *Who?*

"Miss Millie and her family," I signed back. He looked as shocked as I was to find out she was once young and had a family. I started explaining to him about her husband being buried in the cemetery in town but how he had to be buried far in back since the black and the white people had to be separated.

Eddie looked as confused as if I wasn't signing at all. He wrinkled his nose up, making his freckles move on his face. "Why?"

"I don't know. That's how it was back then."

Eddie looked at his own tanned arm like it just grew there and he was seeing it for the first time. Then he signed, "What color?"

Like I said, Eddie usually sees things real clear, so I wasn't sure why he was asking that. "Your skin is white."

He shook his head and his curls bounced. Mama and Daddy used to argue about Eddie's hair. Daddy didn't like it long—said it was too girlie. I think Mama's letting Eddie's hair grow now just to give Daddy another reason to stay when he sees how long she lets it grow.

Eddie continued to shake his head, curls and all, and put his hand on his chest and pulled it away into a fist—the sign for *white*. Then he added, "That window is white. The porch is white. Those flowers are white. My skin is not white. Would some people not like me either? That is stupid."

I rubbed his hair, messing up his curls even more

than they were before and signed, "Everybody loves you, Eddie. But, you're right—it *is* stupid."

. . . . . .

Once Mama got Grandma's house looking and smelling good, she started cleaning out parts of the house most people couldn't see. She was working in the attic right above the room where we slept when I went to put Miss Millie's picture on the dresser beside the rock and the marble.

"Who's down there?" Mama called from the top of the ladder that stretched from the ceiling to the hallway next to our bedroom.

"It's me, Mama!" I yelled back.

"Can you help me with these last few boxes? It is so hot up here, I think I'll call it a day." I climbed up half the ladder to reach the stack of boxes Mama handed to me. Just before I put my foot back on the floor, the boxes tipped, spilling everything out of them.

That's when Grandma walked in.

"Land's sake! Are we cleaning in here or making a mess?"

"Sorry, Grandma." Old photos fell out of one box and a couple of hats fell out of others.

I knew Grandma loved her hats. *A proper lady always*

*wears a good hat,* she'd say—especially when Mama didn't have a hat on her head.

"That was my fault," Mama explained as she came down the ladder, glistening with sweat. "Sorry, Alice. I was in such a hurry to get down from there, I handed you too many boxes at once. It's so hot up there—I need a glass of water—I'll be back to go through all this in a minute."

As she left the room, I prepared to hear a lecture on being messy, but when I looked at Grandma, she was kneeling on the floor looking at the pictures that fell out.

The smile on her face reminded me of the smile Miss Millie had looking at her picture. I wondered if Grandma had all her family pictures in her heart, too, or might those be more things she was forgetting?

I picked up the hatboxes to put the hats back in them, but there were only two hats for three hatboxes. I looked at the empty box, which was the shape of a stop sign with eight sides. It was a pretty golden yellow. On the top of it were the words *Knox New York* and then below two eagles were some other words, MOVEO ET PROFICIO. I had no idea what that meant.

Grandma looked up from the picture she held. I could see it was of Grandpa holding Mama when she was a baby. Grandma's voice cracked a bit when she said,

"Why don't you take that box to store the things you've been keeping on the dresser?"

Could this day get any more surprisin'? Grandma never gave away her things. Maybe her forgetful disease made her forget that?

"Thanks!" I said as I stacked the other two hatboxes on the floor, and headed to the dresser to get the marble, the rock and the picture.

I sat on the bed looking at those things in my new hatbox, thinking about Miss Millie and how nice she was. I knew she didn't like to go to the church here and all, but I kept thinking about her watering Grandma's garden and how Christian-like that was.

I must've been sitting there for a while when Mama came in. I didn't know she was there till she spoke. "What on earth are you dreamin' of with that faraway look on your face?"

I snapped out of my daydream. "Mama, do you think someone can get into heaven even without going to church?"

"I guess I've always believed people have different paths on earth, so why shouldn't there be different paths to get to heaven, too?" She took a drink of her water before adding, "But maybe the most important thing is for people to just be kind." She smiled. "But don't think you're getting out of going to church tomorrow!"

I shook my head. "I wasn't asking for me—I was asking for . . . a friend."

"Alice Ann, honey, it is not your job to have to worry about such things as other people's souls."

It might not be my job, but that didn't mean I didn't want to understand.

Still, Mama's words made me feel a pinch better since I knew that in spite of the unkind things that happened to Miss Millie on the path of life she was walking, she somehow stayed as kind as can be.

chapter **12**

"Well, hello again, Savannah." Reverend Hill smiled at me after service on Sunday.

Poor Grandma looked confused like maybe she'd been mistaken about my name for a while, too. I just stood there, wanting to laugh but feeling guilty.

"I'm sorry," Mama corrected him. "My daughter here is Alice."

He looked surprised and shook his head. "I'm sorry, Alice. I'm usually good with names. Must have you confused with someone else."

"Nice to meet you." I shook his hand quickly and turned to Mama. "I'll go get Eddie from Sunday school." And then I practically ran down the basement steps.

Eddie was happy to see me. Of course, no one in Sunday school spoke sign language, but they seemed to communicate just fine with him. Five different people got Eddie's attention before he left and waved good-bye in a dramatic way. Eddie was grinning from ear to ear. All the way home, he kept telling me about it like Rainbow was a good place to be, not some dried-up little town.

I knew I had to figure out a way to get Daddy to come and take us away before Eddie got too used to everything here.

I headed out back right after church to get the shoe box full of Daddy's letters. Sitting myself down in the grass by the shed, I opened the box on my lap. The musty smell of the first letter I opened made me sneeze. When I blinked my eyes open from the sneeze, I was surprised to see the letter was another poem. Another poem written by Daddy about what he loved about Mama.

And Rainbow.

*On the schoolhouse bleachers*
*during the football game*
*the chill wind warmed*
*when I'd say your name.*

I pulled out another letter. It was another poem.

*A cemetery's bench*
*was never meant for this.*
*But under that old oak tree*
*we shared our first kiss.*

Each and every letter I opened after that turned out to be one more poem written by my daddy.

I tried to think real hard to remember if Daddy ever seemed to like poems when he lived with us, but other than making up silly songs to get me to laugh, I couldn't think of anything like poems from my daddy.

None of it made one lick of sense to me. Especially because those letter-poems made it look like Daddy loved Rainbow. And all Daddy ever talked about as long as I remember him talking at all was that he hated Rainbow.

I wished I had a way to show him these letters. Maybe if he could read them again, he'd remember he loved Rainbow.

And Mama.

And Eddie and me.

But if I told him about the letters, I'd have to admit I was snooping and I knew Mama probably wouldn't like that any more than eavesdropping, so I had to think of some other way to remind Daddy that he really did love Rainbow—and us—once.

That's when it hit me!

What if I went to each of the places he wrote about in his letter-poems and found things—kind of souvenirs—to remind him about the things he used to like? Then, when Daddy came to visit, I'd give them all to him and he would have to remember he once loved Rainbow. And if he remembered he loved Rainbow, he would start to remember loving the rest of us, too.

The possibility of it all made me happier than I'd been in a while.

I read the letter about the wishing well again and at lunch asked Mama if she ever heard of a wishing well in Rainbow. She thought it was a peculiar thing to ask, but remembered there was a wishing well in the park on the street behind the church.

I was getting the bike from the shed to go check out the wishing well when Eddie saw me. "I go, too."

He didn't even know where I was going.

It never mattered to Eddie—he just always wanted to be there. I figured he might as well come, even though I wasn't sure if I was going to tell him what I was doing with the letters and all.

'Course I couldn't ride the bike too fast since Eddie

didn't have one and was walking beside me. I'd ride up the bumpy brick road one or two house-lengths and then double back to wait for him to catch up.

Even though waiting for Eddie to catch up took longer and the Georgia heat grew stronger, we finally made it to the park.

If you could call it a park.

There was a rusty slide and an old swing set with one broken swing and another swing that looked like it would break with the next hint of a breeze.

In the middle of the park there was a spinning thing that Eddie tried to ride on. But when he first touched it, something big and brown and fast ran out from under it and into the nearby bushes.

"What's that?" Eddie signed as his huge eyes followed where that thing ran.

"Rat?" I signed back as I motioned for us to go. Suddenly I didn't care if there was a wishing well there— I just wanted to get away from things that run out from under other things.

But Eddie froze where he stood and pointed to the bushes that lined the park. I followed where he was pointing.

That's when I saw the bushes moving like they were

being blown by a gigantic breeze. But the problem was—there was no wind whatsoever that day in Rainbow. And that meant whatever was moving those bushes was even bigger than what ran out from under the spinning thing.

Eddie and I stood staring at the bushes like our feet were glued to the hard, dry ground under us. My eyes were dang near as big as Eddie's and my heart was pounding something fierce. Finally, the rustling stopped when out stepped a giant . . . girl.

Okay—she wasn't really a giant girl. As a matter of fact it was that same short-haired girl I'd been seeing around town. The waver.

"Hey," she shouted toward us, like she expected us to be there. And of course she waved. "Y'all seen my kitty?"

Eddie laughed so hard at the surprise of the giant rat really being a little girl that he couldn't sign to me what he was trying to sign.

"I think your cat was under that spinning thing and just ran off that way," I told the girl.

"Here Kitty, Kitty, Kitty!" the girl yelled with a trill in her voice.

"What's your kitty's name?" I asked.

She looked at me like I had three heads before she

answered. "It's Kitty, silly! And I'm Pam. I seen y'all around. Y'all livin' here now?"

"No!" I yelled in answer. "We're just visiting our grandma. We live in Columbus."

"Oh . . . I thought—never mind."

As I filled Eddie in on the conversation about the missing kitty, Pam ran over to us.

"Ooh—what's that y'all's doin' there?"

"This is my brother, Eddie. He can't hear, so I sign to him."

Pam walked up to Eddie and yelled right into his left ear. "Are your ears really broken?"

Of course Eddie felt the breath of her words and flinched.

"See—he hears okay!" Pam announced like she had just healed him.

I assured her he really couldn't hear a thing.

"Why?" she asked as she stood in front of Eddie waving her hand *hello* like she couldn't stop even if she wanted to.

Eddie looked embarrassed but waved back.

"He was born that way."

She smiled a sweet smile before yelling again at Eddie: "I AM EIGHT. HOW OLD ARE YOU?"

When she held up eight fingers and pointed to herself, Eddie of course figured it out and held up six.

Again, Pam clapped her hands. "Good! Ya understand! Good boy!"

I decided to let her have her thoughts of miracles as I wandered around looking for the wishing well.

I'd wandered a bit behind the bushes when I heard a meow. When I turned toward the sound, I saw what must be Kitty—sitting right on top of the well.

The well was in a corner of the park, with its stones falling out all around it like it was shedding its skin. I peeked inside it, and as far down as I could see, there was nothing. "Hello!" I shouted down the well, since that's what I thought you did with wells.

My *Hello* didn't really echo, though—it just sort of got swallowed up and disappeared.

I suspected if it really was a wishing well, its main wish might be to get out of that park.

Still, it seemed to be where Daddy was writing about. I pulled the letter from my pocket and read it again.

*The sun's golden rays*
*danced in your hair.*
*You looked in my eyes*

*and asked if I care.*
*How could I explain*
*my feelings so true*
*as I sat there that day*
*by the wishing well with you?*


All of a sudden, I could see Daddy and Mama sitting there as teenagers, so in love. But instead of that making me happy, it made me sad.

Still, I picked up a stone that had broken off from the well. I'd bring it home and save it for Daddy to remind him of happy times in Rainbow.

I called to Pam to get Kitty so Eddie and I could head back to Grandma's house.

"There ya are, silly Kitty!" Pam practically purred to her pet.

I motioned for Eddie that it was time to leave. Pam stopped her purring and looked at me like I was leaving her birthday party right after I got there. "Where y'all going? Don't y'all wanna stay? Or—I can go with y'all, if y'all want . . ."

It was a good thing Eddie couldn't hear 'cause he would've certainly tattled on me for my manners when I just plain as day told Pam, "No."

Just like that. I guess I could've told her I wasn't needing any friends in Rainbow since I wasn't staying long. But I didn't. No explanation to soften it—just *No*.

Have to admit, I did get an uncomfortable feeling in the pit of my stomach when I looked back and saw her standing there looking so sad, holding her Kitty as I rode away.

## chapter 13

Miss Millie had told me I didn't have to walk Clarence on Sunday, but she'd be happy to see me come Monday morning, if it struck my fancy to do so.

Not sure if my fancy was struck or not, but I honest-to-goodness was looking forward to the idea of walking when Monday rolled around.

Since I'd spent a lot of the weekend looking at that picture of her family, I had made up all sorts of stories about her boy and how he died.

Each one of those stories made me sadder than the one before. I needed to know what had happened.

Mama always says people will share their stories on their own time, in their own way, and asking too many questions is just being nosy. So when we started walking, I tried hard to be patient, going on and on about the weather. "I wish they didn't shut down the pool," I complained. "I remember swimming in that pool when I was real little, but Mama said it's closed now."

Miss Millie nodded. "Yep. Everybody lost that fight."

"Whatcha mean?"

"'Member how those laws changed not allowing separate places for black and white folks?" I nodded, and she continued.

"Well, when the law said black folks as well as white folks had the right to swim wherever they wanted, some people got upset. They couldn't agree. Got so ugly, the city just up and closed the pool. Like I said, everybody lost that fight. Dang shame."

"Dang shame . . . ," I agreed.

Thinking about the pool closing, her brother dying and her husband having to be buried in the way back of the cemetery made me so mad. I wanted to know what happened to her boy, but now I was afraid to find out.

But I really needed to know and so I blurted out, "Can I ask what happened to your boy?"

"Umm-hmmm," Miss Millie answered as she continued to walk slow toward the church. Her breathing picked up and I wasn't sure for a moment if I was supposed to ask again.

Before I could come to a decision on the matter, she cleared her throat and began. "Me and Clayton married before James died . . . the year was 1905. Still living in Atlanta. Found out I was with child in '06. James was so excited about being an uncle. Used to talk to my belly and be so funny. Right before he was killed in the riots, he told me he had to go somewhere to make a better world for his niece or nephew. Then he made me promise not to let my baby into the world before he got back."

We reached the church right then and I heard laughing. In the parking lot were the two boys who were in front of Grandma's house last week. I didn't know if Miss Millie could hear and I was sure hoping she didn't since she was in the middle of a story about her boy's short life, and laughter just felt rude.

She paused for a minute and we stood there. The boys were straddling their bikes and the bigger one started yelling and pointing at Miss Millie and me like we were some sort of sideshow at the circus. I couldn't catch what he was saying, but the few words I could make out made it clear not hearing more was a good thing.

I stuck my tongue out at them, holding it there long enough for extra effect.

Miss Millie didn't see me stick out my tongue, but there was no doubt she saw the rudeness of the boys. Still, she didn't seem surprised or mad. She just motioned for us to keep walking.

"Those there boys are the McHale brothers," she told me. "Their daddy, and some others in their family, still don't think black people belong here in this neighborhood—and they like to make sure we know it. We come a far piece, but I guess you can see we have a far piece to go."

I was downright fuming. Miss Millie was in the middle of her memory about her brother going off before he was killed by white folks and all these years later, there were still more white folks stuck in the middle of being stupid.

I didn't want to ask her then to finish her story. I didn't want her to be remembering more sad stuff. But she could tell I was fuming inside.

She walked on and just as matter-of-factly as she said the earlier thing about the McHales, she said, "You don't have to walk with me anymore."

A couple days ago, that would have been great news. I would have run back home, told Mama my job was over and been glad. But not today. Today I wasn't just sad at the thought of stopping the walks, I was confused. All these questions stumbled through my mind. Did she not want to walk with me anymore? Was I proving to be nothing more than a painful memory stirrer-upper?

I had to ask, "Do you want to stop these walks?" The words spilled out with way more emotion than I'd planned. There was even a dang choke in my voice that made my red-from-the-heat cheeks even redder.

Miss Millie smiled. "Alice-girl, I'm used to stuff like that there. Don't particular like it, but I'm used to it. I'm so old and been through so much, ain't nothing people can say or do that can hurt me anymore. But you . . ." This time her voice cracked. "You never been on this side of ugly before. I don't want you shoved across that line on my account."

We walked on. I guess as the distance between the McHale brothers and us grew, the distance between Miss Millie and me kind of shrunk.

I picked my next words as carefully as I would pick flowers in my grandma's garden—if she ever let me. "All I want is for you to finish telling me about your boy."

Miss Millie let out a whistle of a laugh as she shook her head, but I knew she wasn't mad or anything. "Okay then . . . Let's see . . . where'd I leave off?"

"James told you not to have the baby till he got back."

"Ah, yes . . ." She tilted her head like she was going back in time to tell the story once again firsthand. Then she cleared her throat and took a couple deep breaths before she went on. She spoke her words in the direction of the sky like she was telling it to God or something. "Problem was—like ya know—he never come back. Wouldn't ya know . . . the very minute I was told James was killed, my baby chose right then and there to start coming. And he came. Oh, Lordy, he came. James didn't get the time to make the world any better of a place, but my baby came anyway."

Dang it, but my eyes were getting misty again.

"Had me the prettiest baby boy you ever did lay eyes on. Spittin' image of his uncle. So we called him James, just like his uncle."

I wished the story would end right there. I wanted to remember Miss Millie and Mr. Clayton and James all being the family they were in the picture. I wanted that to be the end of the story. But I knew Mr. Clayton Miller was buried under a peeling white cross and baby James was buried someplace else.

"Wh-what happened to baby James?" My voice cracked as my words came out.

Our feet were moving at the same time. Slow, but the same. Right foot, left. Even Clarence was in step with us. When Miss Millie answered, her words were, at first, real soft, and then got loud enough for me to hear.

"Let's see . . . The year was 1911. Me and Clayton and baby James carved out a nice little life for ourselves.

Life wasn't easy, but we got by, trying not to draw too much attention to ourselves. Just be a family. Just be a family . . . Then one night it happened."

When she said those words, my stomach turned like it was getting ready for someone to punch it. I tried to prepare myself for the worst but I suspected there really was nothing that could prepare me for what Miss Millie's life had put her through.

"Baby James was five when he got an awful sore belly. Cried and cried about it. Now, he wasn't one to belly-ache about nothin'. No, he was a brave boy." With these words, her voice filled with emotion. "Such a brave boy. If he fell down, he got back up. If he got a scratch, he never mentioned it. So when this brave little boy said his belly hurt somethin' fierce, I knew it was somethin' bad." She took another deep breath. I think I forgot to breathe.

"After a whole day of that bad belly, a fever started. Then another day of a fever burnin' my baby on the inside. I tried gettin' a doctor to come, but the white doctor refused. I decided to go to the hospital. There was a public hospital in Atlanta, but it was too far. The private hospital was for white people only, but it was closer."

Even after all the things Miss Millie told me, it still felt like a cut to my heart when she said that even hospitals were divided then, too. I shouldn't have been surprised, but I was. Miss Millie knew the question before I asked it and only nodded before she went on.

"Yep. So we took my baby boy to the private hospital hopin' he'd get the help he needed."

By now we were back at her house and she let Clarence off his leash and we sat down at the picnic table. Even though he was released from the leash, Clarence stayed right by Miss Millie's feet.

"The hospital wouldn't take him. Plumb refused. By then my baby was screaming with pain and fever and I plumb refused to leave. They threatened to have me arrested, but I stayed right there with my sick little boy." She let out a deep breath, which sounded to me like life itself being sucked out of her.

"After two hours, a nurse finally let me in and had me wait in a basement for a doctor to see him. It was cold and damp." Her voice grew softer, like each remembered word hurt more than the last. "And . . . it . . . was . . . down . . . there . . . that my little boy . . . drew his last breath . . . in my arms. God rest his soul."

I would later figure it had been over fifty years since that day when Miss Millie lost her baby, but when she was telling me right then, it might as well have been yesterday. The tears in her eyes left the tears in my own eyes no choice but to follow. I reached out to Miss Millie and before you knew it, we were holding hands. And there we sat at the picnic table, the two of us, tears falling like the rain we needed but weren't getting.

I think I heard Clarence sniffle, too.

## chapter 14

Before she got the forgetful disease, Mondays had always been Grandma's bridge day, where her group of lady friends would get together to play cards. But I guess Grandma's bridge-playing days disappeared with her good memory, since her friends hadn't been over in a long time.

Mama hoped a visit from the ladies would be good for Grandma, and I hoped so, too. I have to admit I actually missed Grandma telling me, *Sit up straight* and *Dress more like a lady*. Some days now, she just looks at me like she's trying to remember who I am.

So on that Monday afternoon, when the ladies Mama invited over for a special visit arrived, I decided I'd take a ride on my bike. I knew for once Eddie wouldn't want to join me since he always liked to stay inside where the ladies would feed him all the gingersnaps he wanted.

Mama gave me a dime to buy a Popsicle so I figured I'd head to the General Store after the library.

The librarian seemed like she was waiting for me. "Alice, is that you? My goodness, you've grown this year."

"You, too," I said, but realized soon enough that a lady might not think that was a compliment.

The librarian laughed, though. "I'm Mrs. Davis. I met you a few years back. I went to school with your mama. We even double-dated to senior prom."

"Hi, Mrs. Davis," I answered.

"Looking for anything in particular today—or just browsing?"

"I'm kind of just browsing, I guess." I knew I wanted a poetry book, but I wasn't real sure what kind.

But I soon found what I was after, checked it out and placed the book in the basket of the bike. Then I rode over to the General Store.

Back home in Columbus, I used to love going to the grocery store in the summertime since they had air-conditioning. Walking in there was like walking into a refrigerator.

But I don't think Rainbow has even heard of air-conditioning.

When I arrived, the screen door was propped open like the owner was hoping for a breeze, but instead all he got were some flies and even a stray dog.

I used to think the General Store was kind of cute—with its bins of fruits and vegetables, looking like it wanted to be old-fashioned. But that was before Mama had the idea we were staying here. Now I don't think it's cute at all.

The grocer—I guess the same one whose daughter was out late that night and who got me into trouble for listening to gossip—was shooing the dog out.

"Well, hello, Alice Ann!" he hollered when he saw me, like we were old friends. Does every adult in Rainbow know who I am? And why did he call me by my full name? Only Mama calls me that.

"Hi, Mr.—?"

"O'Brien. You probably remember my dad—he used to run this store, but I've taken over now. I went to school with your mama. I was a couple years older, but I noticed her even then. Everybody noticed your mama. She's a special lady."

I sure didn't like the way Mr. O'Brien was going on and on about Mama. "So you knew my daddy, too, then, right?"

"Oh, yeah . . . Sure. Sure I knew him."

I stood there waiting for him to say how special my daddy was, too, but he wasn't as talkative about Daddy.

"Well," I said. "When Daddy comes, I'm sure he'll want to come say hi to you."

"When he comes?" Mr. O'Brien looked confused. "Oh, sure. That'd be nice, if he comes . . ."

With the grocer done rattling on about my mama and daddy, I went over to the freezer to get a Popsicle. The cold-air blast from the freezer felt good as I searched for a grape Popsicle.

All they had was orange.

Guess nothing in this town was what I wanted it to be.

I gave my dime to Mr. O'Brien and the whole store started shaking with a train going by, so thankfully I didn't have to hear what more he had to say about Mama. But as I walked out, he yelled, "See you later, Alice Ann."

I got outside right when the train finished passing and looked for my bike. I knew I had propped it against the fire hydrant, but it was gone.

I walked around to the left side of the store, so confused I didn't even lick my Popsicle until I felt orange goo dripping down my hand.

I was just about ready to go back into the store when I saw one of those horrible boys—what did Miss Millie say their names were? The McHales! The older McHale boy was standing there with a stupid grin on his face.

"Where is it?" I demanded.

He managed to look even stupider than he usually did. "Where's what?"

"You know exactly what I'm talking about! Now give me my bike!" As I yelled, I pointed my Popsicle at him and the melting ice pop slid off the stick and into the dirt.

"Oh, poor baby! Dropped your little treat. Well, now it's trash just like that piece of trash ya call a bike." He laughed this deep laugh that didn't sound like a laugh should sound at all.

"I swear I'll tell Mr. O'Brien!" Right then I didn't know if I wanted to scream or cry.

"Ooh. A tattletale! That really scares me."

I turned to go back inside, but before I got to the door, the smaller McHale came around the other side of the store with my bike. "Is this yours?" he asked like he didn't know perfectly good and well it was.

"Of course it's mine!" I yelled, grabbing it from him.

"Hey, I didn't take it," he said. "I was bringing it back to ya. I saw it over on the other side . . ."

I'd never really seen this kid up close before. He had reddish-blond hair and freckles like mine. If I didn't know he was a McHale, I might have believed him. But in the short time I'd been in this little town, I'd learned who the McHales were and I didn't like them.

I turned to jump on the bike, but the older McHale wasn't done yet. He grabbed the book in my basket. "Give that back!" I yelled.

"Ooh—what's this?" His voice was sugary sweet as he read the title. "*An Introduction to Poetry*. Do we have a little poet here? Come on—tell me something purdy."

I was fighting back the tears as I tried to get the words to come out, but before I could speak, the younger McHale grabbed the book from his brother and put it back in my basket.

Maybe I should have thanked him, but right then I only wanted out of there.

I hopped on my bike but my foot missed the pedal.

I heard laughter as I finally rode away, pedaling faster and faster, each push of the pedals keeping time with my heavy breathing.

And then I heard it.

Clank . . . clank . . . *clunk!*

And with that sound, my bike chain fell off, making my foot lose its place on the pedal and my whole body lose its place on the bike.

The next second, I felt sharp pains shoot through my

knee, my elbow and my mouth. For a moment I lay on the road all sprawled out.

"Oh my goodness!" I heard a voice coming from down the road. "Y'all okay?"

And there she was—Pam, the girl from the park.

"I . . . I . . . I think I'm okay," I said as I stumbled, trying to stand up.

"Whoa! Let me help ya." In an instant, Pam was off her bike and right beside me.

"You're bleeding," she pointed out in case I didn't know what all the red stuff dripping down my arm and leg was.

I looked at my scratches. Hard to say how deep the cuts were since they were filled with pebbles.

"Y'all want me to go get your mama or daddy or somebody?"

If Pam could get Daddy to come back, all this pain would be worth it. But I didn't want to get into my life story right then, so I just shook my head. "I think I can make it home."

"I don't think your bike can make it home, though."

She was right. Not only was the chain off, but the handlebars were bent and the basket was sort of smashed in. "My book! Where's my book?"

Pam found it a little ways from where I landed and handed it to me.

"I'll walk you home," she offered. "Do ya want to leave your bike here?"

"Nah. I think I can walk it home."

But that was easier said than done.

The *whop-whop-whop* of the bent wheel made even pushing it hard. And considering that my head still felt dizzy and my leg and arm still bled, and that tinny taste in my mouth, it might have been a miracle I was walking at all.

Pam watched me struggle with it. "Here, y'all take my bike and I'll take yours."

After a few minutes of walking our bikes side by side down the road, Pam announced, "Hey, I just realized I don't even know your name!"

"Oh, sorry. I'm Alice."

"Alice!" she exclaimed like there was a bunch of names she'd been pondering for me and that one just won.

When we got to the corner of Grandma's street, I was glad to see the visiting ladies' cars were gone. I sure didn't want all those ladies fussing over me. If I could've, I would've just snuck on in and not told Mama, but Pam had other ideas. "Alice's mama? Alice's mama?" she yelled while we were still in the yard.

I dropped the bike and reached for the door right when Mama opened it. "Alice Ann? Oh, my word, child! What happened?"

Before I could speak, Pam did. "Her chain came off her bike and she fell hard. She's bleeding everywhere."

I just stood there like I was on display. "You poor thing!" Mama looked me over. "We got to get you cleaned up." She opened the door for me to walk in as Pam stood frozen to the ground, looking down. Mama turned back to her. "Thank you so much for helping, young lady. Are you a friend of Alice's?"

"No!" I answered too fast. As much as I hated Rainbow, I sure didn't want Mama thinking I was making friends in it. But I felt bad as soon as I saw the hurt look on Pam's face. "Sorry, I mean, we just really met the other day—but Pam found me when my bike crashed."

Mama smiled. "Well, Pam, it looks like you're a hero today. Would you like to come in and have some gingersnaps while I tend to Alice?"

A person might have thought Mama was asking Pam if she wanted a hundred-dollar reward. The smile on her face started in her eyes and then spread like in slow motion until it was all over. "Sure!" she shouted.

Mama took me into the bathroom to wash out my wounds, which hurt bad enough. But the worst part was when she painted on the iodine to keep out the infection. We both blew on it something fierce to cool it down, but it stung almost as much as falling off my bike.

"I hate those McHale boys!" I said between breaths.

Mama scolded me, but in a softer voice than usual. "Alice Ann, we shouldn't be hating people."

I argued, "But Mama, they make fun of Miss Millie and they hid my bike. Why are the McHales like that?"

Mama shook her head. "I don't really know them so I can't rightly say why they act that way, but I do know that nobody's born hating—they're taught that from someone." She put a bandage on my biggest cut.

I didn't know what to think about that, but when I was done getting bandaged up, I went to look for Pam. I looked in the kitchen where Mama had left her, but no one was there.

I looked in the backyard and the front yard, but still no one.

I peeked in Grandma's sewing room, which was now Eddie's room. And right there on the floor by his cot, in front of Grandma's Singer sewing machine, sat Eddie and Pam, both with their hands over their ears.

"What are you doing?" I asked. But since Eddie can't hear ever and Pam had her ears plugged, no one answered. I did what I always do when I want to get Eddie's attention and he's not looking at me; I stomped my foot on the floor. Both he and Pam looked up at me.

"What are you doing"? I asked again, this time with my hands and voice. Pam kept her ears plugged while Eddie answered. "Don't know. She just came in and started doing that." He shrugged his shoulders. "So me, too." And that made perfect sense to my brother.

I got closer to Pam, who was smiling at me but still covering her ears. "WHAT ARE YOU DOING?" I yelled like she would do.

She yelled back, "I WANTED TO SEE WHAT IT WAS LIKE TO BE DEAF."

Now, that was one of the silliest and yet nicest things I ever did hear. She was pretending to be deaf for Eddie. I don't know why I never once thought of trying it. I sat down beside them and went to plug my ears, too, but then I noticed what Eddie had been showing Pam.

It was my hatbox with Miss Millie's marble, rock and picture.

I scolded in sign language, "That is mine! Not yours. Why is it in here? And why are you showing her?"

Eddie shrugged and tried to smile all innocent.

Pam was watching me sign. "IT REALLY WORKS! I CAN'T HEAR A THING! BUT I STILL DON'T KNOW THAT FINGER-TALKING STUFF."

I pulled her hands off her ears. "You're yelling again."

"Oh, sorry." She looked at the hatbox and picked up the picture. "So did Miss Millie give ya these?"

I nodded.

Pam nodded, too. "Wow. She actually seems . . . *nice* . . ."

"What do you mean?"

"Oh, nothing." Pam couldn't take her eyes off the picture of Miss Millie's family.

I didn't like the way she was holding on to it for so long so I grabbed the picture and the hatbox. "Well, she is nice and all, but this here is my stuff and Eddie shouldn't a went in my room and got it."

Pam said something to me when I left the room, but I didn't want to talk anymore, so I acted like I didn't hear her.

Maybe sometimes I *do* pretend to be deaf.

## chapter 15

"You been in a fight, Alice-girl?" Miss Millie whistled through her teeth when she saw my scraped knee, elbow and chin.

"Yeah," I answered, standing at her back door. "I got in a fight with the road."

"Looks like the road might a won that round." She smiled but not a big smile. "You okay? We don't have to walk today if it hurts ya."

"So this must be Alice!" I heard a voice yell from inside Miss Millie's house. This pretty much surprised me. I only pictured Miss Millie with Clarence—and now me. I guess I didn't really think of her having her own life with friends who stopped by.

"This here lady is Miss Frankie," Miss Millie explained when her friend came to the door. I remembered then that Miss Frankie was the lady on the other end of the party line whose gossip got me to Miss Millie's in the first place.

"Nice to meet you," I said, remembering my manners.

"Pleasure is mine, sweet girl! Pleasure is all mine!" Her voice was twice as loud as Miss Millie's. And she was twice Miss Millie's size, too. The difference in the two friends' size made me smile.

Turning back to Miss Millie, I offered, "If you have company, I can come back later."

Miss Millie laughed. "Miss Frankie's not company. She just stopped by to drop off my cake pan. 'Course she only returns my food containers hopin' I'm gonna fill 'em back up for her with more of my food." She winked at me and smiled at her friend.

Miss Frankie opened her mouth in an exaggerated expression of shock. "Humph!" she said. "Cake needed more salt, if ya ask me." Miss Millie laughed at her friend, who blew her a kiss. "I'm just trying to help ya get that recipe perfect." And before she left she added, "Sure have a hankering for some sweet potato pie, if anybody cares . . ."

Miss Millie shook her head as she turned back to me,

eyeing my cuts and scratches again. "Maybe you should rest today."

I was touched at her worry on my account, but promised I'd be fine and we started in on our usual walk. It's funny how much I'd started to look forward to my walks with Clarence and Miss Millie. Being with them just seemed natural, but I wondered if we made as funny-looking a pair as Miss Millie and Miss Frankie, and if it even mattered.

Lately, I'd been really missing my friend Linda. We promised each other we'd write. I wrote her. Twice. But so far, there weren't any letters from her.

Or anyone.

Maybe it was time to think about making friends here since Grandma didn't seem to be getting any better. Pam was nice—the way she helped me with the bike accident and everything—but I didn't know if that made her my friend. Plus, she was closer to Eddie's age. Was there even anyone here in Rainbow to be friends with?

As we walked past the church, I looked over at Miss Millie and said, "Can I ask you a question?"

She looked straight ahead as she answered. "Free country, last I checked."

I smiled. "Last week, you said you didn't like going to church—"

Miss Millie snorted and turned toward me. "That again? I thought I told ya what I meant."

"No. I know about the 'going to church' thing—but I was wondering—what do you mean about some people being all un-Christian-like? Are there lots of mean people in Rainbow?"

"Alice-girl." Miss Millie shook her head. "The whole world is fulla mean people. But it's also fulla nice people, too. That's the important thing."

I guessed that was true. But it wasn't telling me what I needed to know. "Who's been mean to you at church?"

I didn't hear Miss Millie laughing, but I could see her smile, so I figured she was okay with my question.

"Well . . ." She looked over her shoulder like whoever she was about to talk about might be sneaking up behind us. "There's this one lady . . . never ya mind her name—but she sings in church every Sunday. Every Sunday she's up there singing about what a friend she has in Jesus. 'Course she's singing off-key—but each Sunday she's up there singing and smiling and looking out at everybody like she's the right hand of the Good Lord Himself."

I had to hide my own smile at how worked up she was getting.

She continued. "And after pretending to be the Good

Lord's right hand on Sunday, on Monday, she spreads gossip that would make the devil himself blush."

"Does she gossip about you?"

"Woo–wee!" Miss Millie laughed. "Reckon I'm her favorite subject."

Miss Millie went on. "Ya see, years ago, there was a dear old white lady named Miss Ruth, who lived in the house I live in today. I used to be her maid. She was always real good to me. And when Clayton took sick a year before he died, she let us move in with her. Let us move into her very house! Can ya believe it?"

I didn't know if Miss Millie was wanting me to really tell her if I believed it, but I did. I hoped I would be nice like that if somebody needed my help. And with all the mean white people I knew Miss Millie met in her life, I was real glad to hear there was at least one nice white person in her life. She walked on as she continued her story of Ruth.

"About eight years ago Ruth died. She had no family and left me her house. 'Course some of the neighbors, like that one lady who can't carry a tune in a bucket, were none too happy a colored lady was now their official neighbor; but there it was—writ' out plain for all to see in her last will and testament. So after eighty-some years, I had me a home of my very own." Miss Millie shook her head like she still couldn't believe her luck. "Yessiree. Ruth was a true, true friend. God rest her soul."

Miss Millie stopped walking for a minute, so I figured you had to stop in order to get a soul blessed by God. I stopped, too. I noticed Clarence sat down, maybe even lowering his head like he was saying a little prayer.

When the moment of blessing was over, Miss Millie started walking again. "Yessiree, after Miss Ruth died, that there lady didn't like me living in her neighborhood at all. And I think that there lady had an actual thought so infrequent that when she did get one, she had to share it with everyone around to make sure she didn't lose it. So I stopped going to church most Sundays."

My head moved up and down like I understood, but I still had a question. "I thought you told me yesterday that you were too old to let things hurt you anymore."

That's when I saw her whole face smile. She reached out and touched my shoulder. "Ah, Alice-girl, truth be told, you're never too old to be hurt just a little. But if you're lucky, one day you be smart enough to quit putting yourself in the situations that hurt ya."

By then we were back in Miss Millie's backyard. She asked me to wait a minute while she went into her house. I bent down to pet Clarence, who rolled over, showing me his belly so I'd rub it.

A few rubs later, Miss Millie was back. "Wanted to show ya this here. Miss Ruth give it to me." She opened her hand, which held a little pink-and-tan shell. "Ruth told me it's called a scallop shell. See how it fans out like that?"

I nodded.

"Ruth said that represents all the different journeys everyone takes in life—but see how it all meets up at this point?" She pointed to the top of the shell. "That's to show we might all come from different directions, but hopefully, we all end up at the same place one day."

"That's real nice," I said, surprised my voice was almost a whisper. "That Miss Ruth was real nice."

Miss Millie nodded as she put the shell in my hand and folded my fingers around it. "She sure was." She patted my hand. "She sure was."

## chapter 16

Pam must've loved being called a hero, 'cause after my mama called her that, she started to come over pretty near every day. After the first couple of days, Mama didn't even have to ask Pam if she wanted to stay for lunch, we just knew she'd eat with us.

In a short while, Pam found a way of communicating with Eddie. It was less like sign language and more like charades, but it worked for them.

Most days she'd start by playing with Eddie, but eventually she'd end up playing with me or both of us.

One morning she asked about the tire swing on the ground. "Why don't ya hang that thing back up in the tree?"

I shrugged. "It's too heavy to lift."

"If we lift it together, it'd be easier." She said that like we were a team, always trying things together. Yet somehow it didn't sound wrong.

Eddie dropped his plate to help us try to lift the tire back up to the chain but it was still too heavy.

I signed to Eddie, "Go get the wheelbarrow in the shed."

He disappeared for a few minutes and came back grinning at his accomplishment, pushing the dirty wheelbarrow.

"Good!" Pam clapped her hands together, like that was a sign.

I shook my head. "No, you say 'good' like this. Put your right hand up to your mouth. Now move it straight down to meet your left hand."

Pam tried it as Eddie nodded his head and clapped for her.

"I know a sign!" she shouted. "Thank you for teaching me that one."

I smiled at her excitement. "That's pretty much the way you sign 'thank you,' too."

She squealed. "I know *two* signs!"

When she and Eddie stopped telling each other "Good" and "Thank you," I rolled the tire into the wheelbarrow while Pam held it steady and Eddie pulled the chain around the tire to connect it to the chain from the tree.

"We did it!" Pam yelled, signing "Good" over and over again to the tree.

Since Eddie wasn't one to celebrate too long, he picked his plate back up and, in a sign everybody knew, waved his hand toward himself to tell Pam to go with him.

I hopped on the tire swing to test it out and watched Pam explain through her motions that Eddie's "bus" needed to stop at another tree. Eddie stopped and Pam went to the tree, acting like she was buying something. Then she licked a make-believe ice cream cone and handed another make-believe cone to Eddie. It was silly, but I kind of wanted her to hand me a make-believe cone, too.

When I got tired of watching their game, I headed back to the shed and Daddy's letters.

Pam must have eventually tired of the game, too, because a few minutes later she joined me.

Eddie still had no interest in the letters from Daddy. But Pam sure was interested.

"So your daddy wrote these letters to your mama? They're so pretty. I don't think my daddy ever wrote anything pretty to my mama. Or anyone."

"At least you get to see your daddy all the time."

But that actually made her look sad. "Yeah—he's around all the time . . ." She looked back at the letter in her hand. "Why did your daddy leave after writin' these pretty words?"

"Well, he wrote these a long time ago. But he's coming back soon. I'm just getting things together to show him when he gets here to remind him of these places he loved. And Mama."

"Does your mama know ya found her letters?"

"Umm . . . no. And . . . it's a surprise for her, too—so don't tell her, okay?"

Pam squealed with excitement. "I love surprises! And I'm really good at keepin' secrets, too. I mean, last week, I saw my brother break the front window of our house when he threw a baseball and he told me not to tell *no one* and I never told no one. Well—I never told no one till right now."

I couldn't help but smile at her before turning to read again the letter-poem I was holding. "This one is about the schoolhouse and the bleachers. Is that close by here?"

Pam squealed again. "Yes! I know where that is! It's not far from here! I can show ya! I can show ya right now!"

She motioned for Eddie to come as I yelled into the house that we were going on a walk.

We passed the church and the street that led to the park and the wishing well.

Then Pam led us to another road I hadn't been on yet. This one dead-ended into a building that had a sign out front that said, RAINBOW JUNIOR AND SENIOR HIGH SCHOOL.

The combination school looked to be as falling apart and lonely as the park and the wishing well. And the whole town.

"Ta-da!" Pam exclaimed, like she was pointing to something other than a run-down old school.

I tried to muster up some pretend approval for this place. "Thanks for bringing us. Um . . . are there bleachers here somewhere?"

"Of course, silly!" Pam slapped Eddie on the back like he was in on the joke. Eddie saw her laughing and started laughing, too. "The bleachers, of course, are in the back by the football field. C'mon, I'll take y'all there."

When Eddie saw the lines of the football field, he smiled like he'd found the most perfect road for his pretend driving. He started driving his plate up and down those lines while Pam ran behind him as the perfect passenger, moving everywhere he moved, stopping every time he stopped.

I walked over to the sad-looking bleachers and tried

to imagine what they were like when my daddy put his arm around my mama here. I sat down and opened up the letter-poem Daddy wrote about Mama when they were there so long ago.

*On the schoolhouse bleachers*
*during the football game*
*the chill wind warmed*
*when I'd say your name.*

With the sweat dripping down my back and the heat of the sun on the bleachers coming through my shorts, it was as hard to think of a chill wind as it was to think of my daddy writing that poem for my mama and her name.

If I squinted I could imagine Mama sitting next to me on the bleachers, smiling her smile. But no matter how hard I tried, I couldn't see Daddy sitting there next to Mama.

And before I knew it, I had tears in my eyes. Shaking my head, I tried to blink away the dang wetness in my eyes.

I was hoping to find something to represent the bleachers to show to Daddy when he came, so I started to look around. Under the bleachers I could see trash and rocks and a couple of things that were moving. Still, nothing looked special enough to stir up the memory I needed stirred.

But then I saw it!

A little ways down from where I was sitting, there was a triangle flag on a stick. As I got closer to it, I could see the flag was red and white and had the letters *RHS*—for Rainbow High School, I guessed.

As I bent to pick it up, I noticed it was a little dirty—actually very dirty—but I could wash it in the sink before giving it to Daddy.

I sat on the hot bleachers holding the dirty flag while my brother and Pam zigged and zagged on the football field. As I watched them laugh and communicate in their own made-up language with the words *good* and *thank you* being signed as much as possible, I realized Rainbow was becoming home for Eddie now. And it scared me that it was starting to feel like home to me, too. I felt guilty, like I was betraying Daddy.

All at once I couldn't take a deep breath. It was like an elephant was sitting on my chest—a big old elephant named Rainbow. And that elephant would only move if Daddy came back.

I was counting on my collection of stuff to help with that. But then it hit me—maybe my collection was also to remind me of him.

Was I was forgetting Daddy?

Daddy's laugh? I couldn't hear it anymore.

Daddy's face? Blurry.

I knew I had to get him to come back as soon as possible.

I reached in the pocket of my shorts and pulled out another one of Daddy's letter-poems. I read it a couple of times, not liking at all where it meant I had to go.

But I knew I didn't have a choice.

## chapter 17

I waved my arms in the air to get Eddie's attention as I yelled to Pam, "I have to go to the cemetery!"

"What?!" Pam yelled back.

"The cemetery! I need to go there now!"

Pam walked over to me. "Did ya say y'all want to go to the *cemetery*? Now? Why y'all want to go there?"

"It's another letter. There's a bench in the cemetery where Daddy sat with Mama and they had their first kiss. I need to go find it and bring back something from there to show to Daddy to remind him."

"What's your hurry?" Pam asked.

I didn't want to tell Pam that I couldn't picture Daddy anymore. Couldn't bring myself to say out loud I was forgetting him.

My heart was beating louder as I climbed down from the bleachers. Still, I heard Pam's voice loud and clear. "Don't ya think your daddy would come if he wanted to?"

I walked over to her, my face feeling hotter with every word. How could she say that? Her daddy's home all the time. What does she know about how it feels to forget your own daddy? "You can't understand! This will work! My daddy just needs to be reminded how he used to feel and it has to be soon!"

By now, Eddie was waiting for me to interpret what we were saying but I couldn't stop long enough to sign.

I turned and started running to the cemetery like my life depended upon it.

When I got to the big iron gate, I stopped dead in my tracks.

I was so mad I hadn't figured out what it would take to really go into the cemetery by myself. I looked around the gate. Maybe there was a bench outside the cemetery that could be their bench.

But no such luck.

I had to go in and get to that bench.

My heart was beating so fast I was getting dizzy.

I wished Miss Millie was here. I remembered how easy she walked in that gate and all the way to the back of the cemetery to see her Clayton.

I put one foot in front of the other and went inside the gate.

Then I heard something.

It was a crunching noise. Something was moving.

And it was getting closer to me.

Right then a shadow fell over me and I screamed.

"What ya screamin' for?" a bicycle rider asked me.

But it wasn't just any rider. It was one of those McHale brothers. The younger one.

"I wasn't screaming," I answered.

"Well, it sure enough sounded like a scream. Ain't y'all never seen a bike in a cemetery before?" he said, and started laughing.

"I'm not talking to you." I continued walking deeper into the cemetery.

"Well. I was talkin' to you. Y'all don't gotta be so mean."

I couldn't believe that! One of the McHale brothers telling me not to be mean!

But before I could muster up a comeback, Eddie and Pam came running up the cemetery path. "What ya doing here, Pam?" the McHale boy asked.

"Me and Eddie was chasing Alice—but she's really fast. Eddie couldn't drive that fast. What you doing here?"

"Just riding my bike." He looked back at me like he wanted to say something, but instead he just shook his head.

He turned back to Pam and mumbled, "Don't be late coming home. Dad was in one of his moods when I left the house—so don't make him madder by being late. Again."

With that, he jumped on his bike and left.

"*Dad*?" I said, and turned to Pam.

"Yes." Pam spoke slowly, assuming Eddie could read her lips. "THAT IS MY BROTHER." Eddie nodded like that made all the sense in the world.

"So if he's your brother, that would make you a . . . *McHale*?"

"Yep. Pamela Lyn McHale, at your service." With her last words, she bowed.

"But . . . but . . ." I didn't know exactly how to ask this in a polite way. "Isn't everyone in your family mean?"

Okay. Maybe there wasn't a bit of politeness in that question. But still, I wondered.

Pam kind of laughed, but it wasn't the happy giggle I'd grown used to. "No, silly! Now, my—my daddy gets really . . . mad sometimes . . . and he can be kinda mean. Mama says he's under a lot of pressure looking for a job.

And my oldest brother—he tries to be like Daddy. But my other brother—that one there who just left . . . he's nice. Real nice."

I remembered Miss Millie telling me about the McHales' daddy not wanting black people in his neighborhood. So I had to agree with Pam that her daddy could be mean—but I wasn't ready to agree with her about even one of her brothers being nice—but just as I opened my mouth to say so, I saw it.

It was a bench. Nestled under a big oak tree in the middle of the cemetery. It had to be Mama and Daddy's bench.

I walked over to it and ran my fingers over the roughness of the wrought-iron bench where Mama and Daddy had their first kiss. I sat down and pulled out the other letter in my pocket and read it out loud.

*"A cemetery's bench*
*was never meant for this.*
*But under that old oak tree*
*we shared our first kiss."*

Eddie read over my shoulder and then put his finger next to his nose, with a twisting motion—the sign for *boring*—before picking up his plate and driving it around the paths. Pam sat next to me and smiled at the words. "That's one of my favorite poems. Does your daddy still write poems?"

I had no idea what Daddy did anymore, but I didn't need to admit that, so I just told Pam, "Sure. He's real good at lots of things."

I would've liked to tell Pam all the things Daddy was good at—helping me with my math homework, teaching Eddie to tie his shoes, or me to play checkers or tell jokes. But the truth was, Daddy hadn't helped us or played with us in longer than I could remember. Last Christmas he stopped by to tell Eddie and me he'd bring us our presents later. But he never did. Even before Daddy left our house over a year ago, he'd changed.

But I just knew I could change him back.

I tried to look around for something—anything to remind Daddy of this bench and that kiss. Pam was looking around, too, but I don't think she understood what she was looking for.

Just then, though, she said, "Look at this leaf. It's bigger than my two hands put together. It might be the biggest leaf ever."

"That's an oak leaf," I told her—proud I remembered what Grandma told me about the one in her yard.

But then it hit me. "An oak leaf! That's it!"

"That's what?" Pam looked confused.

"Mama and Daddy sat under this very oak tree to have their first kiss! So what better thing to remind Daddy of that kiss and those feelings than a big old oak leaf from the tree? Pam—you're a genius!"

Pam lit up with one of those big smiles that took over her whole face. She even puffed up her chest a bit, too.

I felt closer to Daddy already just sitting there on their bench and the cemetery didn't seem so scary after all.

I knew it wouldn't be long before he would fall in love with Rainbow and Mama and us all over again.

And so, armed with the flag and the leaf, we all three marched home.

## chapter 18

"I got the job!" Mama announced as she hung up the phone.

"What job, Joanie?" Grandma asked. "Or did you already tell me?"

Poor Grandma. On her bad days, she couldn't remember things. But on her good days, she couldn't forget not remembering.

But maybe I was getting forgetful, too, 'cause I had no idea what Mama was talking about either.

"I didn't want to say anything earlier," Mama explained, "in case I didn't get the job. But that was Gloria Davis, my friend from high school who's a librarian. I'm going to work at the library!"

"Why do you need to get a job here?" I asked Mama, who was practically dancing around the room. "If you need a job, why don't you just ask to get your old job back in Columbus?"

In Ohio, Mama had worked as a school secretary. She'd pretty much worked ever since I could remember, unlike Daddy. Sometimes he wouldn't go to work at all. Other times, he'd be gone a few days, saying he was starting something big.

Mama stopped her happy-dance and looked at me, sighing more dramatic than usual. "Alice, I'm getting a job here at the library to help support us. It'll be a good thing and it's just down the street."

"Well, congratulations, honey," Grandma said. "I'm just sorry you have to get a job. Seems like you always had to be the one working before, too."

With all Grandma's forgetting lately, it was funny how she could remember just fine that Daddy didn't work much when he was home.

Eddie tapped Mama on the shoulder to ask what was going on.

When she told him her news, he asked, "What about us?" Then he signed, "Who will stay with us?"

Mama nodded and signed, "As long as Grandma is

having a good day, like today, I think Alice can help her enough to stay with you. If it looks like it's a bad day for Grandma, I'll stay home. Gloria—Mrs. Davis—knows all about Grandma. If something happens, I can be home in two minutes. Is that okay with you, Alice?"

"Not really." I looked down and stared at the kitchen table with the white crocheted tablecloth Grandma made. I pulled on a loose piece of yarn that was looking like it was ready to escape the rest of the tablecloth.

"Alice Ann, we have to make a life for ourselves here."

"We have a life in Columbus." I pulled the yarn and the rest of the tablecloth puckered and rose up like a magic trick. I could tell Mama was signing something in silence to Eddie, but I didn't look up to see what it was. Eddie signed something back and then left the room.

"Is it really that bad for you here?" Mama's voice was soft, but it cracked a little.

I shrugged.

I was just about ready to tell Mama how much I was missing Linda, my school, my daddy, when someone was knocking at the door. Since the screen was open, I could see it was a man. Again, for a second, I thought it was Daddy.

"Pat!" Mama practically laughed as she stood up

from the table, fixing her hair like she was gonna get her picture taken all of a sudden. "What a nice surprise to see you today!"

When he came in the door, I recognized him as the grocer but couldn't figure out why he was here at our house and why Mama was so happy to see him. He sure wasn't carrying any groceries with him.

"Hi, Joanie. You look lovely today." I was scowling at him when he turned to me. "And so do you, Alice Ann."

I just stared back without answering, but seeing Mama's eyes glaring at me, I knew I had to mind my manners. "Thank you, Mr. O'Brien."

"Your mama told me about your bike accident, and, well, my daughter, Maddie, has a bike she's too big for now. So I brought it for you."

He opened up the door and waved for us to follow him outside where there was a bike that was a lot better-looking than Mama's old bike. It was a green banana bike with a long flowered seat. I fought the urge to take it for a ride since I didn't want Mr. O'Brien thinking I liked it. Or him. I remembered the last time I heard about his daughter. "Is Maddie still seeing the son of the post office guy?"

The look on his face made me smile, but Mama's look told me I'd gone too far.

"Um . . . no . . . they aren't seeing each other anymore."

He looked back at Mama, who cleared her throat before talking. "Alice, did you *forget something?*"

"Thank you for the bike. I don't think I'll need it, but thanks."

Mama shook her head at me and motioned for them to go back inside.

I just stayed on that porch, looking at a bike that— like everything else—didn't really belong to me.

chapter **19**

The heat of the end of June made me honest-to-goodness miss the heat of the beginning of June. When I walked outside it was like wandering smack into a baker's oven that got cranked up a degree or two with each slam of the door. Even with Grandma's two box fans, it wasn't much more comfortable inside.

Every night, after I prayed for that blasted heat to let up some, I prayed that Daddy would come or send word he was coming the next day. Figured I had my bases covered then. Surely God would answer at least one of my prayers. But every morning it just got hotter and the messages from Daddy never came. I started to worry that maybe God was as deaf as Eddie.

But on the first of July I woke up early feeling extra-hot and extra-sticky since Mama got up before me to get ready for work and took the fan with her.

I was too hot and sticky to get dressed, so I walked downstairs in my pj's to find Mama sitting at the kitchen table reading a letter. Mama saw me and tucked the letter under her book. "Good morning. You're up early."

I yawned and sat next to her. "Couldn't sleep. It's so hot here."

"Oh, I'm sorry—I took the fan. You can have it back if you want to go back to bed for a while." Mama's eyes darted to the book that was covering the letter.

I nodded toward the book. "Who's the letter from?"

Mama pulled it out from under the book. I glanced at the envelope hoping it was signed *SWAK*.

It wasn't. But I recognized Daddy's handwriting and a wave of happiness blew over me, which felt better than a thousand fans.

And then I saw Mama wipe her eyes. I hoped with every ounce of hopefulness I had inside that those were tears of joy because the letter said he missed us something fierce and wanted us back in Ohio. But from the sour look on her face, I sort of knew that wasn't the case.

I reached for the letter, but Mama pulled her hand

and the letter back. "There's . . . um . . . there's a lot of boring details in here, but"—she cleared her throat again and tried to sound happier—"but he said he's going to try to visit Rainbow."

"When? When is Daddy coming?!" I yelled as I threw my arms around Mama.

"Now, Alice Ann," she said, "you have to remember Daddy sometimes makes promises—"

"When? When did he say he's coming here?"

She took a deep breath before she answered, "The Fourth of July. He said he'd be here on the Fourth of July."

Maybe I should have asked her then and there why that answer-to-my-prayers news would make her even a little sad, but I couldn't bring myself to think anything but happy thoughts. My daddy was coming in three days.

Three days!

Independence Day would be a perfect day for him to come and break us all free of Rainbow.

· · · · · ·

"Is my clock wrong, or are ya early?" Miss Millie stood at her back door, dressed in her usual shirt and jeans, but with her hair not in its usual braid. Her silver hair hung in long strands, making her look younger even with all her wrinkles.

I walked on in, noticing Clarence didn't even bark to announce my arrival. "Sorry I'm so early, but I couldn't wait to tell you—Daddy's coming home! I mean Daddy's coming here—in three days, on the Fourth of July!"

"Is that so?" Miss Millie said. "Well, I'll be . . ."

"Yep. He wrote to Mama and told her that very thing. He's gonna come here and remember he loves us and never want to be without us anymore."

"Said all that in a letter?"

"Well, not exactly. I don't rightly know what all he said in the letter. Mama was kinda tearful and emotional about it. But he's coming and I know it's all gonna be okay after that." I thought of all the treasures I had collected and tucked away in Mama's box of letters— treasures I would be giving to Daddy in just three days!

Miss Millie nodded as she ran her fingers through her hair like a comb. "How's your little brother feel about it all? Is he excited your daddy's coming?"

"Not really," I admitted. "Eddie feels things different. When I told him at breakfast that Daddy was coming, he just looked at me like I'd told him I was eating a dang egg for breakfast."

"Hmmm." Miss Millie was now braiding her hair while looking straight at me. "Do you think he doesn't want your daddy to come fetch y'all?"

"I don't know. When I asked him if he misses Daddy, he said the darndest thing—he just said, 'Not really.' Can you believe that?"

But before Miss Millie could say anything, Eddie was standing at her door, holding his plate. "Well, wonders never cease! Look who's here." Miss Millie waved hello to him.

Then he turned to me. "I walk with you today, remember?"

In my excitement to tell Miss Millie about Daddy, I forgot I'd promised Eddie he could walk with us today. He liked the excuse to "drive" his plate farther than Grandma's yard. "Sorry," I signed, rubbing my fist over my heart.

"Right," he signed back. And while he can't make his voice show sarcasm, he does a really good job of it with his face.

So the three of us . . . well, four of us . . . started our walk. Then Miss Millie asked, "How's your grammy doing lately?"

"Hard to say," I told Miss Millie. "It changes every day. Last week she had three good days in a row. And then it was like a switch got turned off in her head. She just forgets everything. Like yesterday she insisted on making her usual Fourth of July cookies with red, white and blue icing that she makes every year, even though Mama told her it was too early to bake 'em. She made 'em anyhow and she must've mixed up the sugar with the salt in the recipe 'cause they looked something awful and tasted even worse."

Miss Millie shook her head. "That's a dang shame."

"Dang shame." I nodded in agreement.

I heard a car coming from behind us, slowing down. The man driving hollered, "Well, hello, Mrs. Miller. Good to see you feeling better."

Miss Millie cleared her throat to answer. "Morning, Dr. Watkins. Ya know I'm too ornery to stay down for long."

The doctor smiled a real nice smile at Miss Millie.

Eddie was now waving—but not to the driver—he was waving to the passenger, a girl with brown hair and pigtails. She was smiling at Eddie and waving back. Then she looked over at me looking at her and we waved to each other, too.

"Well, you two, try to keep my patient here from getting into trouble," the doctor told us. "Heaven knows I can't." And with that he grinned and drove off.

When they left, my brother signed, "Who?"

I signed back, "Miss Millie's doctor." Eddie nodded but then stopped to ask another question.

I translated for him. "Eddie wants to know if you're sick."

Instead of telling me what to sign to Eddie, Miss Millie looked right at him and shook her head. Then she pretended she had a cane and could barely walk. "Just oooooold," she answered in an exaggerated way.

Eddie laughed so hard he dropped his plate. Miss Millie looked pleased she was able to talk to Eddie all by herself. "Bless his heart!" She grinned.

But after she took a few more steps, and coughed more, I asked, "Are you sure you're not sick?"

Miss Millie smiled at me. "Like I told Eddie, I'm old, Alice-girl. And truth be told, when you're ninety-two, ya know ya can't be long for this world."

I knew Miss Millie was old. And I knew she coughed all the time. But hearing her say that made my heart hurt. She looked over at me. "Now don't be scrunchin' up your pretty face on my account. Whatever happens to me next, I'll be ready. Don't ya fret none. Now tell me more about your daddy coming here."

She knew that would make me change the subject, and it did.

## chapter 20

I woke up earlier than even Mama on the Fourth of July. Truth be told, I don't think I slept much at all.

Daddy was coming!

It'd been so long since I'd even talked to him, which was why I wasn't sure I remembered his voice. About a month before we moved, he called and asked me about school, but he was asking about my teacher from back in third grade. Whenever I'd ask Mama if I could call him, she'd say he was traveling and she didn't have a number for him.

We'd spent the day before cleaning. Even though Grandma's house wasn't that big, it took all day to dust and sweep and scrub it. And even though Grandma's house is really old, I sat there that morning, smiling, thinking it looked pretty good. I hoped Daddy would smile when he saw the house and us.

After rereading all his letter-poems about being happy here, I was sure Daddy couldn't really hate Rainbow.

Maybe I didn't hate it as much either.

All that mattered though was that he remembered how much he loved us so that we'd be together again, wherever we lived.

I got dressed in my blue shorts and my red shirt and as soon as Mama got up, I had her put my hair in braids with red, white and blue ribbons. When I saw myself in the bathroom mirror, I wondered if I was still the spittin' image of Daddy.

I couldn't wait to find out.

As it got closer and closer to the time of the parade, I couldn't stop smiling. My face felt funny with all that happiness holding it together.

Sitting on the porch, I was planning on how the day would go. First, we'd go to the parade. Then we'd walk back to Grandma's house, where we'd have our picnic. Mama was inside already getting things started and the smells coming from the house made my tummy rumble.

After our picnic, I'd have Daddy go into the back-yard with me. Just the two of us. That's when I'd show him the letter-poems I found and the treasures I collected for him.

And what would happen next, I couldn't quite imagine, but I knew it would end with more hugs and smiles.

Pam came over a little before the parade started. "Where is he? Where's your daddy?"

"He's not here yet," I admitted, looking down the street, hoping to see a car that might be his.

"He better hurry. The parade starts in a few minutes." Pam saw Eddie inside and opened the door to just go on in.

I made sure she heard me when I yelled, "Don't worry! He'll make it."

But he didn't.

......

When Mama, Eddie and Pam were ready to leave, I told Mama I'd stay and wait for Daddy.

But she wasn't hearing it. "No," she told me. "You need to come with us. We won't be far—just right up the street. He'll know where we are if he gets here before it's over."

So even though I wasn't with Daddy, I agreed to go to the parade.

Of course, calling it a parade might be a bit of an

exaggeration. There was the one police car starting things off, followed by a group of adults wearing ribbons across their chest with titles like *Mayor* and *Grand Marshal*. After them came what I guessed was the high school marching band. And then there were a bunch of bicycles decorated with red, white and blue streamers. One boy put playing cards in his bike's spokes, trying to make as much noise as the drumbeat had before.

Finally, there was a fire truck that said *Centerville* on the side, with some firemen standing on it, waving to the crowd. Turns out Rainbow's so small they had to borrow a fire truck from somewhere else for a parade. Guess they'd have to borrow it for a fire, too.

As we watched the parade, I felt the sweat dripping down my back. Everyone always said you get used to this heat after a while, but if that's true, I want to know how long a while is.

I guess the heat is the only thing Rainbow doesn't do small.

While I was feeling like a sticky pile of clothes being held up by a sweaty mound of flesh, I glanced at Mama and wondered if we were even related. How could she look so fresh-as-a-daisy pretty on a sweltering day like today? Lately I'd been noticing she looked extra-nice.

And I wasn't the only person noticing.

That dang Mr. O'Brien came over to watch the parade with us, which didn't make me happy at all. What if Daddy came back right then and thought the wrong thing? And the way Mama was giggling at everything the grocer said that wasn't even funny, I could see that Daddy might be right in thinking the wrong thing.

. . . . . .

As soon as the parade was over, I ran ahead of everyone to get back to Grandma's house. I stopped running when I saw there wasn't an extra car in the driveway.

I peeked in the screen door just to make sure he wasn't inside, maybe took the train, but the house was quiet. By the time everyone else got back from the parade, I was sitting in the shade on the front porch swing, waiting. Mama looked at me with sad eyes that made me think maybe she was missing Daddy, too.

I guess not sleeping much the night before, combined with the rocking motion, started to make my eyes flutter shut and before I knew it, I plumb fell asleep in that rocking chair.

The next thing I knew, there was a tap on my shoulder. Maybe I was dreaming about Daddy, because I just knew I'd see him tapping me when I opened my eyes. But it was only Eddie. The disappointment tumbled from my heart to my stomach and I had to blink a couple of times to focus on what he was signing. "Daddy on the phone."

That made no sense. Why was he on the phone when he was on his way here?

I raced inside to hear Mama arguing with him. "I can't believe you are doing this. Again. No, you tell her . . ."

Mama handed the phone to me.

"Daddy? Where are you?"

"Hey, baby-girl! How is my beautiful baby-girl?"

"Where are you, Daddy? You already missed the parade. It wasn't much, but you missed it! When are you coming?"

The silence on the other end made my heart sink.

"Daddy?"

"I'm here."

"Where? Where are you? In Columbus?"

"No . . . I'm not in Columbus anymore."

My heart filled with hope. "Well, Daddy, when you get here, I have a surprise for you. I think you're really going to like it. Are you almost here?"

He cleared his throat. "Baby-girl, I'm in Las Vegas."

Now, I knew that was west of here, far west of here. And I also knew it meant Daddy wasn't coming. Words kept pouring out of the receiver, tumbling straight to the floor, but it was like they were in another language. I did hear some words like, ". . . great city . . . job opportunity . . . call you soon . . ." They rattled around my brain—but nothing made sense and my attention began to fade until I heard an odd but familiar coughing in the background of the phone.

I hung up. On Daddy. Never did that before. Hung up on the same daddy I'd been waiting to talk to for so long.

Mama saw and didn't tell me anything like *It's rude to hang up without saying goodbye.* She just tried to hug me—but I shook loose of her and started walking . . . one foot in front of the other . . . until I found myself at that shed.

I picked up the old shoe box of letters with the heart and Mama's and Daddy's names scribbled inside it. I opened it and saw the letters with the rock from the wishing well, the school flag, the oak leaf, an old picture of the two of them at their prom that Grandma had, and everything else I'd collected.

And right then I did the only thing I could think of.

I threw the box back in the shed, not even stopping to worry about everything inside scattering all over the floor.

After that, I put one foot in front of the other once again until I found myself at Miss Millie's.

## chapter 21

Miss Millie sat at the picnic table. And beside her was Miss Frankie working her way through a plate of food.

Mama would have said it was horrible manners to barge in when I saw Miss Millie had company. But I couldn't help myself.

I stomped over to the picnic table that was full of enough chicken, potato salad, deviled eggs and chips to feed a lot more than the two ladies, and plopped myself down.

Just like that, I sat down like they were waiting for me and it was about time I got there.

Miss Millie looked over to me and tried to smile, but her smile didn't look too happy.

"Glad you're here, Alice-girl," she finally said.

But I couldn't begin to talk just then since I had more emotions swirling inside me than Miss Frankie had piles of food on her plate.

And that was a lot.

Miss Millie cleared her throat. "Miss Frankie, I reckon you remember Miss Alice, here?"

Miss Frankie nodded my way, and I was glad to see she was too busy eating to want to chat now.

Which was fine with me.

I was done talking to people.

Maybe forever.

Miss Millie looked at Miss Frankie and moved her head up and down like she was waiting for something. Miss Frankie shrugged her shoulders.

Then Miss Millie cleared her throat again, this time real dramatic-like, the way a person does when they really don't have something stuck in there, they're just trying to get someone's attention. "Ahem!" she said to Miss Frankie, before she turned to me. "Alice-girl, I think Miss Frankie owes you an apology."

Miss Frankie snorted, stopped her chewing and wiped her mouth. Finally, in an exaggerated fancy voice, she said, "Miss Alice, I do so beg your pardon. When the phone rang a bit ago, I's in the house fetching a fork—

'cause some people don't know how to set a table—well, I's fetching myself a fork when that phone rang. Thinking it was for Millie, and being the thoughtful friend I am, knowing how much older she is than me, I grabbed that phone. Guess it wasn't for Miss Millie, though—it was for you. It was your papa."

So that was it. When Daddy was coughing up excuses, I thought I'd heard actual coughing that sounded like Miss Millie on the other end. So I guess this time it was Miss Frankie doing the listening in on the party line.

Miss Millie, who I noticed still hadn't touched her plate, turned back to me. "I'm so sorry your daddy didn't come today. Do ya want to go inside and talk? Or maybe we could take Clarence for a walk after dinner—where is that dog? Can't believe he's not begging for food."

Before I could answer, we were interrupted by a boy standing at the open side gate yelling, "I think he belongs to you, don't he?"

I don't know if I was more surprised that the boy who was doing the yelling was none other than the younger McHale brother—or that the "he" he was referring to was Clarence.

Clarence—who wasn't moving at all!

"What did you do to him?" I shouted as I ran over to them. I wanted to smack that McHale boy, but Clarence took up the entire length of his arms and I didn't want to accidentally hit the dog instead. So I started pumping my clenched fist in the air, pretending I was hitting that boy, and maybe even Daddy, Mama and everyone in Rainbow, too.

Miss Millie, who I guess has had a lot more practice dealing with sadness and disappointment, raised herself from the picnic table and walked over to Clarence. "What happened to my dog, young man?"

The McHale boy had the look of a lamb who'd accidentally wandered into a den full of foxes.

"I . . . uh . . . found him up the street. A car . . . It didn't stop."

At that moment I prayed to the God I hoped wasn't deaf at all. I prayed that Clarence wasn't dead. Hadn't Miss Millie lost enough in this world?

The thought of that ornery little dog not running in circles anymore made my eyes start to water, too.

Would you believe right then and there I knew God could hear just fine since Clarence started to stir in the McHale boy's arms? His wrinkled eye peeked open as he let out a low pathetic growl like he was telling the McHale boy he wasn't as helpless as he looked. Miss Millie took Clarence in her arms and he yelped.

"Musta knocked him out, but he seems to be coming to." She moved to the table with all the food and scooted the fried chicken and deviled eggs to the side so she could lay down her little baby. Miss Frankie's eyes grew as big as those deviled eggs at the suggestion of her Independence Day feast being ruined, but even she knew not to interrupt Miss Millie right then.

The rest of us stood back and watched as Miss Millie stroked the beat-up tan-and-white hair of her Clarence and looked for injuries. His tiny circle eyes peeked out from his tan eye patch and watched her every move like he was saying, *It's okay, I trust you.* I saw her lips moving, but couldn't hear the words she was saying to him as she, ever so gentle, felt around his whole body. When she got to his hind leg, he let out another yelp.

I looked over at the McHale boy, who stood there with his mouth wide open and his arms still reaching out like he still held Clarence.

Miss Millie pulled out her handkerchief and wrapped it tight around Clarence's hind leg, knotting it with the skill of someone who'd done such a thing before. When she was done, Clarence licked her hand, like he was saying, *Thanks, that's better.*

Then he must've got a whiff of the feast laid out next

to him, because he turned his head like someone called his name, stood up on all but his hind leg and started to eat a chicken leg.

At the sight of the dog eating her feast, Miss Frankie let out a yelp like she'd been hit by a car as well. To keep the peace, Miss Millie moved Clarence with both his sore leg and his chicken leg to the ground. Then she turned to the McHale boy. "You got a first name, Mr. McHale?"

"I . . . uh . . . yes."

"Well, do I have to guess what it is, or might ya tell me?" Miss Millie winked at me as I remembered my similar first encounter with her.

"I . . . um . . . My name is Jake."

"Well, Jake, I owe ya for saving my dog. Thank ya kindly." With those words, she stretched out her hand to shake his. In that moment, fear crept across his face as if he was staring at a poisonous snake about to strike and not the hand of an old lady.

I've heard grown-ups talk about time standing still, and I never got it before. But right then at that moment when Miss Millie held out her hand to Jake McHale and he wasn't sure what to do with it, if time didn't stand completely still, it at least slowed down more than a bit.

Even Miss Frankie stopped slurping up her food.

And I swear Clarence paused from his bone to watch the goings-on.

At the moment time might have been remembering to go forward, Miss Millie might have been remembering just who was on the other end of her stretched-out hand. I was remembering what I heard about the McHales' daddy being mean and prejudiced, and Miss Frankie saying, *The apple doesn't fall far from the tree*, right when Miss Millie might have been thinking all that, too. I saw the smile begin to leave her face as her hand began to lower.

But right before her outstretched hand came to rest at her side, Jake McHale reached out his dirt-covered hand and grabbed Miss Millie's hand in his.

"You're welcome," he managed to say as he pumped their hands up and down.

The smile found its way back to Miss Millie's face and when the handshake pumping was over, time got back to ticking away at a regular speed.

"Guess Clarence wandered off through the gate *somebody* left open." Miss Millie looked directly at Miss Frankie, who had resumed her consuming of the feast. "Whereabouts did ya find him?"

"Up by the church," Jake answered, not taking his eyes off Clarence. "He kind of was runnin' in circles up the street when a car come by. They screeched their brakes, but hit him hard enough so's he couldn't move. Then the car up and left."

"And ya saved him and brought him back to me. Thank you." Miss Millie was trying to sound all conversational, but she was starting to sound more emotional at the suggestion of Clarence just lying in the street.

A blush washed over Jake's freckles, blending them all into one big patch of red splashed across his face.

"Well, the least I can do is give ya some food for your troubles," Miss Millie offered to the boy, who gulped at the suggestion. From the looks of him, he didn't get a lot of offers to eat.

And right then on that holiday, standing beside Miss Millie's picnic table, I was looking at that skinny Jake McHale and thinking about Pam saying how mad their daddy got and I started wondering what kind of rough life they had.

All he seemed to be doing was eyeing the feast on the picnic table. He stammered, "Oh—oh, I couldn't—" He looked toward the front yard like he was looking for somebody or some reason, but whatever reasons his head had for saying no, his stomach seemed to overrule them and his whole body just plain sat down and started eating a drumstick like it was the last drumstick on the planet.

Miss Millie laughed and handed him a plate. Then she turned to me. "Alice-girl, why'nt you join us, too?"

I really wanted to, but I knew Mama would be looking for me soon to come to our own picnic. So I sat down and decided to just nibble on a handful of potato chips.

I was thinking as I looked around at that picnic table, we sure made an interesting Fourth of July party. But once everybody started eating, it all seemed kinda natural.

But before I could reach for more chips, Miss Millie's picnic was interrupted once again—this time when someone yelled a word that would get my mouth washed out with soap if I even whispered it. We all turned to the front gate to see the older McHale brother, who yelled, "What do ya think you're doin'? Sittin' with . . . *those people*? Eatin' *their* food? Wait till Pa hears about this!"

Jake turned pale and jumped up from the table so fast, he fell. Picking himself up, he ran out of the backyard, not once looking back.

After Jake and his brother left, we didn't feel like eating anymore.

Except for Miss Frankie, of course.

chapter **22**

I didn't feel like playing much the next day, but the house was just too hot to stay inside. On the tire swing, in the shade of the tree, I could at least feel a little breeze blowing as I was swinging back and forth.

Pam was over and playing checkers with Eddie. But even she seemed quieter than usual—which for Pam was huge.

Swinging gentle in the tire, I tried to forget how mad I was at Daddy.

I watched Pam and Eddie play their game. When Eddie won, Pam signed "Good." He, of course, signed "Thank you." Then I couldn't believe it, but I saw Pam fingerspelling her name to him. Her hand shook way too much for good fingerspelling, but Eddie didn't seem to mind. He signed "Good" over and over to her.

I watched Eddie start "driving" again while Pam folded the checkerboard back into the box. It didn't fit just right and I saw her get madder at it until she finally just tossed the checkerboard on the ground. That wasn't like Pam.

I walked over to her. "You okay?"

She looked embarrassed and said, "I'm fine, silly! I'm fine . . . fine . . . fine."

And wouldn't you know that was one *fine* too many? I saw Pam's bottom lip quiver before she began to cry something fierce.

"I . . . I have to go. Daddy . . . was mad . . . and poor Jake . . . and . . ." She moved to get up, but it looked like her legs weren't letting her. Instead she just cried more.

I sank down next to her and all I could think to do was pat the top of her head. It kind of looked like I was petting Clarence and it must have felt the same to Pam.

She smiled through her tears. "I'm not a dog, silly."

I lowered my hand so it rested on her shoulder. "What's wrong with Jake?" I asked. I mean, he did save Clarence and all. It was only polite to ask.

She looked at her hands, stained with dirt and

scratches. "Remember when y'all said my family was mean?"

How could I forget? "I'm sorry—and you know I didn't mean you—you're nice."

She sniffled again. "I know, silly. But y'all is right. My daddy sure is mean. He was yelling at me today and Jake told him to stop. But Daddy doesn't like to be told what to do."

"Is your brother okay?"

She nodded her head up and down but didn't stop crying. "But sometimes I don't like my daddy very much. I know it don't seem right, but it's true."

Didn't that beat all? After I'd spent all day thinking about how mad I was at my daddy, Pam started telling me more about how upset she was with hers. Through her tears, she used words like, "Smacks us . . . yells at Mama or Jake when they try to stop him . . ."

By the time she was done telling about her daddy, we sure could've used Miss Millie's hankie. Instead, Pam had to use the bottom of her shirt. We both laughed at that.

After Eddie came back to play with Pam, I sat for a while by myself and had me a revelation. Like another closed window in my brain was cracked open with new information again. Maybe, just maybe, having no daddy was better than having a mean daddy.

My head started spinning from all the new thoughts cramming into it. I was confused and knew where I needed to be.

. . . . . .

"Do you think Clarence is okay to walk?" I asked a surprised Miss Millie as I stood at her back door. We'd decided to let his hind leg rest and not walk him that day, but I really needed the company now, and Clarence was standing next to her, looking fine.

"He's doing so much better today—wants to be up and moving even though he still limps a bit. I'll bet it'd do him good to get out for a stretch."

We were almost at the church before Miss Millie said, "Do you want to talk about it?"

I shrugged.

She whistled through her teeth. "Well, if ya drag your feet any more, I think people will think you're older than me." She chuckled just enough to start her into a coughing fit.

I walked on without saying anything.

"That's fine," she offered. "Sometimes we just need to

be alone in our thoughts." She looked at me again. "But sometimes we just need to remember we're not alone."

We walked a few more steps before I finally spoke. "My birthday's next month."

She whistled again. "Well, goodness! I sure understand why you're so upset about that—what with ya being so very old and all."

I rolled my eyes. "It's not that. It's just with what happened yesterday, I don't think Daddy will even remember."

"Hmmm." Miss Millie nodded. "You afraid he'll forget your birthday? Or you afraid he'll forget you?"

That's when my own tears started. "Both."

Miss Millie stopped walking and put her arm around me. Clarence walked until his leash tightened and he jerked his head a little in the tug of it. He looked back at us and before I knew it, he was nudging his head on my hand like he wanted me to pet him all of a sudden.

That made me snort through my tears.

Miss Millie took out a new hankie and wiped my eyes. "I promise ya, Alice-girl, your daddy is the one missing out the most by not knowing the real you."

Before I could answer, I saw a lady I recognized from the choir walking out of the church, heading our way. I thought it might be the one who Miss Millie said gossiped about her. But I wasn't certain.

Until I heard the two ladies together.

"Millllllllie." The lady held out her name for pretty near ten seconds, saying it as sweet as one could.

Miss Millie wasn't participating in the sweetness. She said the lady's name like she was taking attendance. "Miss Mary."

Miss Mary continued being her overly friendly self. "And this precious child must be Loretta's granddaughter. I heard you two were becoming quite the twosome. Two peas in a pod, I hear."

"This here is Alice. Alice, this here is Miss Mary, the one I was telling you about who sings in church."

I tried not to laugh out loud at Miss Millie's message to me, and Miss Mary didn't seem to notice there wasn't really a compliment in there for her. "Oh, that's so nice of you. I do my best. For Him." She paused and looked up to the sky.

Miss Millie turned to start walking again, but Miss Mary stopped her. "Actually, I'm glad ya mentioned that—I've been meaning to tell ya, I was speaking to the preacher about your funeral."

Miss Millie nodded her head. "Yeah, I bet ya were."

Miss Mary smiled an overly big smile. "Well, I heard ya in there the other day discussing it with him—so I told him it'd be my pleasure to sing when the day comes."

Miss Millie tipped her head back and looked down her nose at Miss Mary. "Well, aren't you just a little singing vulture—waiting for me to die."

"Oh—no, of course not!" Miss Mary pretended to be shocked. "I certainly hope it's not for a long time. But know when it happens, I'll be here."

"That's what keeps me living," Miss Millie mumbled as we walked away.

I glanced back at Miss Mary, who no longer pretended to smile.

We walked only a few more steps before I had to ask, "Are you dying?"

"Alice-girl, we all are dying."

We walked on. "You know what I mean."

"Yes."

"Yes, you know what I mean—or yes, you're dying?"

Without missing a beat, she answered, "Both."

## chapter 23

Later that week, when Mama was working and Eddie was watching television, Grandma was holding a book like she was reading it, but for the whole time I watched her, she wasn't turning any pages.

She saw me staring.

"Land's sake, Alice, it's impolite to stare. Go play—ride your bike or something."

Maybe riding that bike of Mr. O'Brien's wasn't a bad idea. "Are you sure?"

She stood up. "As a matter of fact, my head hurts a bit. I think I'll go lie down. Eddie's glued to the TV, so don't worry about us. But be sure to comb your hair before going outside. It looks like a rat's nest in the back."

I hadn't heard that side of Grandma for so long, it might've been the first time her being critical made me smile.

I decided it *was* time to ride that bike. I still didn't have to keep it, but I figured it wouldn't hurt to ride it a couple of places like the library.

It actually was pretty nice. Rode much better than Mama's old one. But I wouldn't tell Mr. O'Brien that. Not yet.

Just when I turned the corner off Grandma's street, I saw that Jake McHale out tossing a ball and running to catch it all by himself. It was the first time since the Fourth of July that I'd seen him. As I was riding my bike past him, he looked up and saw me and hollered my name. Just like we were old friends.

I stopped my bike and looked around to make sure that the bigger McHale brother and the daddy weren't around. The coast was clear.

"How's the dog doing?" he asked.

"His name's Clarence," I answered.

"How's Clarence?" he tried again.

"Good."

"Did y'all get a new bike?"

"Sort of—well, no, not really—well, kind of," I stammered.

He laughed, but it wasn't a mean kind of laugh. It was a nice kind of laugh. "Well, I wish I'd sort of, not really—well—kind of get a nice bike like that."

I have no idea why but he smiled real big at me then. And I have even less of an idea why I smiled back.

Then I got on my kind-of new bike and headed to the library.

......

Nobody saw me walking in the door. I went over to a tall stack of returned books and noticed the book on top was a sign language dictionary. I remembered Pam's finger-spelling and had to smile, picturing her working so hard to talk to Eddie.

I was looking for Mama to tell her about Pam learning sign language when I heard her voice from behind some shelves, talking to Mrs. Davis.

"I just don't know what to do anymore. I can come to terms with him being out of my life. But the kids—it's not right for them."

I stopped in my tracks so Mama wouldn't know I'd overheard that. And she went on.

"He never calls. Never! Is it so hard to pick up a phone and talk to your daughter?"

Those words might as well have slapped me across

my face. I stepped back and looked away to try and stop the tears that were forming in my eyes.

I noticed a girl with pigtails who looked kind of familiar sitting at a table reading a book. Right when I looked at her, she looked at me, too, and smiled. I was embarrassed what with her seeing me all emotional, but there was something nice about her and I nodded. Still, I couldn't even begin to smile back at her, especially after what my mama said next.

"I don't know what to tell the kids. He just keeps saying he's trying to find himself."

I ran out of the library, jumped back on the bike and pedaled like I was being chased. Or maybe I was chasing something—and I was tired of it. So Daddy was trying to find himself? Well, good luck to him, 'cause I sure hadn't been able to find him for a long time!

Finally getting back to Grandma's, I dropped the bike and ran to the shed in the backyard. I grabbed the letters that were still scattered on the floor.

And then I grabbed a shovel.

I walked to Grandma's garden, where the soil was softer, and I started to dig a hole. But the shovel wasn't digging deep enough and fast enough for me so I dropped it and started to dig with my hands. I must've looked like a dog getting ready to bury a bone, but I didn't care. I dug and dug until my fingernails were sealed with dirt.

When the hole was finally deep enough, the sweat was dripping down my face so much I could barely see—but I managed to pour all Daddy's love letters in the hole and cover them up.

Daddy buried all those feelings a long time ago. It only seemed right that those letters get buried, too.

## chapter 24

A crash came from the house followed by the sound of glass shattering.

I ran into the kitchen and heard the commotion coming from Grandma's room. Eddie saw me run in and followed me into Grandma's room.

We found her standing in front of a broken mirror, her hands raised to her face, bright red blood dripping from one hand down her arm and onto the floor.

"Grandma!?" I hollered.

Eddie started to walk closer to her, but I motioned for him to stop because of all the glass on the floor. Watching my step and walking more careful than I'd ever walked before, I made my way to Grandma.

Grandma looked at me like she was a little girl and I was going to scold her for breaking the mirror. "I'm sorry," was all she could say. Over and over. "I'm sorry . . ."

"It's okay, Grandma. Please sit down and I'll try to help you."

I didn't know whether to try to clean up the glass so no one else got hurt by it, or clean up Grandma's bleeding hand first. My head and heart were racing.

"Mother?" Relief washed over me when I heard my mama's voice calling to Grandma.

Mama grabbed a towel and tiptoed over the glass to help Grandma, who was sitting on the bed now, stammering about how the woman in the mirror scared her, and how she had hit the mirror to make that strange old lady go away.

"Don't worry, it's okay," Mama said in a soft voice, soothing Grandma.

I was standing next to Eddie, who held tight to my waist as we watched Mama finish wrapping Grandma's hand.

Once Mama had stopped the bleeding, she led Grandma around the glass and toward the door, saying to me, "Sweetie, I'm gonna take Grandma to Dr. Reilly. If he's not there, I might have to take her to a hospital to get her cut checked out. We'll talk when I get back. I heard you were at the library—that's why I came home early. Honey, I'm so sorry . . ."

Eddie and I followed them outside and watched the car pull out of the driveway. I started to let a tear fall, but saw that Eddie was scared and was looking at me like I was the last person he had. And I guessed maybe I was.

I signed to him that everything was going to be okay— Grandma would be fine and Mama would be home soon.

Maybe if I told him that enough, I'd start to believe it, too.

. . . . . .

Eddie and I had been in the backyard for less than half an hour when the sky changed.

One minute it was a normal hot and sticky Georgia summer afternoon. And the next the wind started blowing this air that made the trees move like they were dancing in rhythm. Then it grew as dark as I'd seen it get before bedtime, looking like nature knew what was coming and decided it was time to cut off the lights for a bigger effect.

Maybe nature knew what was happening, but I sure didn't.

And neither did Eddie.

He's a pretty tough little guy. I guess maybe not hearing the scary things in life makes him less fearful. But when the world looks like it might be ending, I suppose that is even scarier when you can't hear.

As soon as the wind started blowing, he grabbed me, sticking as close to me as one person could stick to another without completely becoming that person.

I tried to walk with him in that position so we could get back inside, but it was dang-near impossible.

Because there hadn't been any rain, the ground was nothing but a mixture of dried leaves, brown grass, clay and dust. And as soon as the wind started to blow, everything on the ground got lifted into the air and stirred up like it was in a huge Georgia blender.

Something flew into Eddie's eye. He screamed like his eye had just been poked out as he let go of me and cupped his hands over his entire face.

It's not easy to reason with Eddie when he's upset, but when a boy who "listens" with his eyes can't see, there is no use to even try.

Still, I tried to get him to come toward the house with me.

That's when I heard the sound of rain coming like the roar of an engine over my screaming brother. And no sooner did I hear it than I saw it and felt it. Instead of just rain, it felt more like heaven opening to spill every-thing and everybody back to earth.

And while this was happening, Eddie started run-ning with his eyes clenched shut—in circles. I would've laughed at how it reminded me of Clarence running blind in a circle the way he does sometimes—but I wasn't in a laughing mood.

I knew we needed to get inside fast but now the wind was blowing so fierce and the rain was falling so hard I could only see a few feet in front of me in the dark and Eddie wasn't there.

There was no point in hollering for him. And as scared as I was for me, I was ten times more scared for him to be running mostly blind and completely deaf in this storm.

Then a flash of lightning hit and the lights that were on in Grandma's house were gone.

Gone, too, was the wind and the rain. All at once, everything was quiet.

Real quiet.

Too quiet.

I stood froze to the ground, not knowing what to do.

That's when I did the only thing I could do.

I started to yell.

All the frustration and disappointment that I'd swallowed all these months seemed to come out at once. It started in my toes and rose up and out of me like a volcano waiting to release lava it'd been holding for years.

I screamed and screamed.

And then, over my own wails, I heard a familiar voice. "Hey, Alice-girl!"

I stopped screaming. I didn't see her but I could hear her. "Ya gonna just stand there and blow away or ya wanna come join your brother and me inside?"

## chapter 25

Never had I been so happy to hear that crackling voice. I squinted into the wind and walked toward the direction of her voice. "Miss Millie? Eddie's with *you*?"

"As sure as I stand here, he plumb jumped the fence and ran right into my house and into my arms, he did. I figured someone had to be looking for him."

"Yes, ma'am. Mama had to take Grandma to the hospital." I started explaining when I saw Miss Millie at the fence, but she interrupted me.

"Maybe you can tell me all about it inside the house. We don't get many tornadoes in these here parts, but I'm not likin' the looks of those clouds."

And at the mention of tornado, I, too, was inside Miss Millie's house and practically in her arms.

When I got inside, Eddie was curled up with Clarence. As soon as Eddie saw me, he ran to me. I could see his eyes were red from whatever had got stuck in there.

But I guess my eyes were red, too.

"I think we'll all be fine, but just to be safe, we should go down to the cellar."

Now, I like cellars about as much as I used to like cemeteries, but I like the idea of a tornado even less, so me and Eddie and Clarence all followed her.

The cellar smelled musty and I sneezed the second we got to the last step. From the candle Miss Millie held, I could see nothing but cobwebs and canning jars. I was getting ready to say maybe we didn't have to be in a cellar when I heard the rattle of the wind against the cellar door that led to the outside. The wind was knocking so hard it was like it was demanding to come in.

Miss Millie led the way to a couple of chairs. "Here ya go. Little dusty, but it'll do."

I sat down on a chair, and Eddie again almost climbed into my skin.

Then, Miss Millie, with Clarence right at her feet, sat down. As soon as she did, Eddie leaped off my lap and climbed into Miss Millie's lap. Miss Millie smiled and her eyes glistened as he buried his head into her chest and shut his eyes.

The wind continued to knock at the cellar door as my brother clung to Miss Millie and she stroked the curls on his head like I imagined she used to do to her own little boy so long ago.

Then she looked at me. "Ya need a blanket? That rain gotcha good."

I felt a chill from being wet as soon as Eddie left my lap, but I wasn't in any mood to be comforted, so I just shrugged and answered, "Nah."

Miss Millie continued to stroke Eddie's hair as she looked at me with a sad smile. "So what's got ya so upset tonight?"

I still wasn't ready to talk. I shrugged. "I don't like tornadoes."

"Oh, fiddlesticks! That's not the reason, Alice-girl. Now, tell me the truth. When I saw ya outside you were cursin' at the heavens. And believe me, I know cursin' at the heavens when I see it. What's got ya?"

I folded my legs up so that I could wrap my arms around them, resting my chin on my knees. I stared at Miss Millie, but said nothing.

"All righty then, if ya want us to sit here and stare at each other, guess I got nothin' better to do."

She stared back with such a concentrated expression, I had to look away before I did something I didn't want to do, like smile.

But in spite of wanting to wallow in my bad mood a while longer, I guess I needed to talk even more.

So I looked back at her.

And told her.

I told her about Eddie getting hurt and running away and me being scared.

I told her about Grandma breaking the mirror and cutting her hand.

I told her about all Daddy's broken promises and the buried letters.

I told her about Daddy looking for himself and me looking for him, too.

And I told her I might have finally realized that Grandma wasn't ever getting better and Daddy wasn't ever coming back.

· · · · · ·

And near the end of my telling, I heard the wind stop knocking. I heard the soft sound of Eddie's snoring. And then when I was done telling, I heard Miss Millie.

"Alice-girl, ya know one thing I learned with all my disappointments and loss?"

I shook my head.

"I learned it's okay to get mad. It's okay to get sad, but after all that gettin' mad and sad, ya gotta get smart. Ya gotta take a step back, away from all your hurtin', and figure out what ya can change and what ya can't."

I sat there, listening, kind of wishin' I had that blanket after all. But I wasn't ready to admit Miss Millie was right about that, or any of it.

She cleared her throat and continued, talking soft, shielding Eddie's ears, like she forgot he couldn't hear. "Sweetie, I don't know your daddy from Adam, but I have to say you're not gonna change him. A leopard don't change his spots. Seems like he's moving on with his life. Maybe one day he'll realize what amazing kids he's missing out on knowin', but until then, ya can't worry about him so much ya waste the love of the people around ya."

I heard Miss Millie continue on. "And your mama, I think she's doin' the best she can. For you, for this little guy, for her sick mama. Just like you're doin' the best ya can. We're all in this great big world just bumpin' around each other trying to do the best we can . . ." Her voice trailed off a bit. I knew her breathing was getting heavier. She was starting to wheeze again from all the talking.

I watched her there with Eddie curled up on her lap

in the damp musty cellar. I watched her still stroking his hair, all soft-like, all the while she was trying to make me feel better. I let her words come into my ears and rattle right through me before I wiped my eyes on my still-wet shirt.

The lights started to flicker back on, and I was thinking the storm was officially over. I wondered if Mama would be home and thinking we got blown away in the storm.

Miss Millie must've read my mind. "Wonder if we need to get you two back before your mama gets home and worries herself to death. I think it's safe now. Feel better?"

There was still a lot I wasn't happy about. There was still stuff I didn't like. But if I thought real hard, the kind where your thinking goes all the way down to your soul, I had to admit, I did feel a little better.

## chapter 26

"Happy birthday, dear *Alice, happy birthday to you!*"

As the singing and the signing of the birthday song ended, I took a breath before blowing out the eleven candles. "Make a good wish!" Pam yelled.

It's funny. I knew exactly what I would've wished for a month ago. But like I feared, Daddy didn't remember it was my birthday with a card or a call or anything. I figured I'd used up enough of my wishes on him.

I shut my eyes and blew.

"Yay!" Everyone clapped.

"What'd y'all wish for?" Pam asked. "Nah, don't tell me—it won't come true!"

Mama pulled the cake back to cut it and serve it to my guests: Pam, Eddie, Miss Millie, Clarence, Mrs. Davis, and even Mr. O'Brien, who I told Mama could come.

Grandma was here, too. She hadn't needed stitches but her hand was still bandaged from her accident. She seemed perfectly happy to be sitting between Miss Millie and Mrs. Davis, like she was enjoying my party just fine.

"First piece goes to the birthday girl!" Mama announced, bringing me the corner piece of the chocolate cake.

"Thanks, Mama." She smiled at me and nodded to Clarence. "Looks like someone is enjoying one of your presents."

One thing I asked for for my birthday was a new dog toy. When I first told Mama that, she thought I meant I wanted a stuffed dog. But I explained I wanted a chew toy for Clarence.

After I opened it and gave him a toy shoe that squeaked, Clarence got real close to it and sniffed it. Then he looked up at me like he was insulted. He might have even rolled his eyes. But after I threw it and squeaked it and chased it myself a few times, he figured it out and started wagging his tail like he was enjoying it.

When everyone finished their cake, I walked into the living room where the grown-ups had gone to sit. I came in on the end of Mama and Miss Millie's conversation.

"But don't tell her what I said or her head will swell so big she won't never be able to leave the house through the door again." Miss Millie laughed, and coughed a bit.

Mama laughed, too. "Well, thank you for those kind words, and I agree, my daughter is a great young lady. But I have to thank *you*, Miss Millie. Your friendship has meant so much to her—to us."

I knew Miss Millie didn't like to get all mushy and she really didn't like getting compliments, so I waited to see what she'd say. She shrugged her shoulders until they looked like they were stuck around her ears as she looked right at me and winked. "Who said nothin' good never comes from eavesdroppin'?"

Everybody laughed and soon Miss Millie was coughing.

"Want a drink of water?" Mr. O'Brien asked as he stood up and walked to the kitchen. Miss Millie shook her head, but Mama nodded to him that it was a good idea.

They didn't understand Miss Millie's coughing fits like I did.

I followed Mr. O'Brien into the kitchen.

I didn't mind him being around so much anymore. Especially after he'd asked Mama to teach him some sign language. But I had to laugh when he tried to sign to tell Eddie something was funny and it looked more like he had something stuck on his nose.

Still, it was nice he was trying.

Before he brought the drink to Miss Millie, who wasn't coughing anymore, I had something I needed to say. I cleared my throat. "Um . . . thank you for the bike, Mr. O'Brien. It's real nice and I like riding it around town."

"You are very welcome, Alice Ann—I mean Alice." He smiled at me. "I'm glad you could get some use out of it. Are you having a good birthday?"

I looked around my house and saw all the people—and of course Clarence—there. I had to admit I was having a pretty good birthday after all.

And I smiled. It was good to be eleven. I already knew so much more than when I was just ten. Lots of living and growing must make a person smarter.

I looked at Miss Millie and figured she'd been living and growing for ninety-two years. I guessed it was no wonder she was so smart.

## chapter 27

On my next walk with Miss Millie, who was waiting for us on the corner, straddling his beat-up bike, but Jake McHale.

Miss Millie nodded to him. "Mr. Jake."

Jake looked over his shoulder like he was afraid a mountain lion might jump out at any minute.

"Hi, Mrs. Miller . . . um . . . Alice."

I nodded to him. "Hi, Jake."

He continued his yammering, looking mostly at Miss Millie. "I . . . I'm sorry my brother . . . my dad . . . what they say ain't what . . . I want to say."

Miss Millie moved closer to him. I wondered if she was seeing his freckles, his sad eyes, his scratches or maybe she was just seeing Jake. "It takes a strong plant to come up out of the hardened ground, 'specially when it ain't given much sunshine."

Jake looked right back into her eyes and smiled a smile that said he knew she wasn't really talking about growing plants. They were having themselves a moment.

Then Miss Millie brought me into their moment. "Ain't that right, Alice-girl?"

I was okay with their moment going on and I was old enough to understand what Miss Millie was telling Jake. But I was staying quiet, still wondering what kind of hardened ground their home was built on, when Miss Millie repeated, "Ain't that right, Alice-girl?" And then she started coughing.

I'd grown used to those coughing fits. Didn't like one bit how frequent they were, but I knew to wait it out.

Poor Jake didn't know that. He hopped off his bike like he was gonna have to catch Miss Millie if she fell. "Can I get ya something?" She shook her head as he turned to me. "Is she okay?"

"She'll be okay—she's used to it. We just need to give her a minute." Miss Millie cleared her throat as the coughing let up.

Jake smiled a scared kind of smile. I noticed all his smiles seem kind of scared.

"Where's Pam this morning?" I asked him.

Jake grinned bigger at his sister's name. "She checked out another sign language book and is studying that thing all the time now. Taught me a couple things, too." When he said that, he shrugged and looked away like he was embarrassed.

Clarence started whining at the delay in the walk. Jake nodded to him. "Good to see him walking normal again. Clarence, right?"

Miss Millie nodded. "Wouldn't have happened without ya carin' for him, Jake."

That was enough to make him turn completely red as he hopped back on his bike and waved. "I'd better get on home. See ya later." And then just to seal the deal, he yelled back, "Bye, Alice!"

"Bye, Jake!" Miss Millie and me both said at the same time. I looked at her and she was grinning like she knew something I didn't.

"He's a good egg, Alice-girl. Him and Pam—and maybe, maybe someday even the older, angry one—they just need some friends, too. Everybody does."

Of course I was okay with being friends with Pam. And Jake, too—but now Miss Millie was even suggesting I could be friends one day with the McHale I knew was as mean as his daddy? The same one I knew was a rotten egg? Maybe all that coughing had finally gone to her head.

"Alice-girl," Miss Millie began as if I spoke my last thoughts out loud, "sometimes we have to take the high road. 'Specially with children who only be imitatin' what they been taught."

Before I could figure out what to say back to her, we reached a street where we usually turned left instead of right.

Today she wanted to go down the other street.

Now, even though I'd been in Rainbow almost three months and had gone to church, the school, the park, the library, and of course on lots of walks with Miss Millie, I had to say I hadn't been up and down all the roads in the town. And that one was new to me.

Miss Millie stopped in front of a pretty house with a big front porch and a sign that read JOE WATKINS, M.D. "I need to go in here. I'll only be a minute. How 'bout you and Clarence wait on the porch?"

This was strange, but the porch was nice. It was in the shade and there were pretty yellow flowers with dark middles that I saw on a lot of porches here. Black-eyed Susans: I remembered Grandma once told me their names.

Clarence and I were just sitting there on the porch swing when a girl about my age came out.

She had pigtails and a real nice smile that looked familiar. She just stood there like I was supposed to know who she was. "Hi?" I said, realizing it sounded like the question it was.

"Hi," the pigtailed girl said. She looked almost as awkward as I was feeling. "I'm Charlene."

"I'm Alice."

"I know."

"You know? Do you go to my church?"

"No." She smiled but the awkwardness was kind of going away with her smile. "No—my daddy's a doctor and Miss Millie told me about you last week when she was here."

Then I remembered the car that stopped, with the girl in it waving to Eddie and me. And that's why the pigtailed girl who smiled at me at the library looked familiar. I started to nod.

"Miss Millie said you're eleven, too," Charlene said.

"Yep—just had a birthday last week."

"My birthday was last month!"

We talked about the library and school and birthdays for a few more minutes before Miss Millie came back grinning like she had a secret.

Before we started walking again, I told Charlene maybe I'd see her later.

When we got about a block away, I finally said, "I know what you were doing back there."

"Wh-what? Visiting my . . . my doctor?" Miss Millie sputtered all innocent-like.

"Uh-huh. All that talk about needing friends . . . Do you think you have to find friends for me?"

"Well, somebody better!" As she said that she laughed and began to cough again. We had to stop completely. Finally, she was done coughing, but she wasn't yet done talking.

"Alice-girl, ya need more friends."

"I got you."

Those dang words jumped out of my mouth before I had a chance to think about them. When I heard them, I was embarrassed that I sounded like a whiny little girl.

Miss Millie smiled a real nice smile though and just said, "That's real sweet, Alice-girl. But I don't have much longer."

There it was again.

Since that walk when she told me she was dying, I didn't want to talk about it, but sometimes she'd say things like how she just knew Miss Frankie would cause a scene at her funeral or how Miss Mary would want to sing. Every time she'd say something like that, I'd change the subject. But there was something about the way she was talking and the way she was looking at me: I just knew this was different. My heart felt all sad but I couldn't change the subject this time.

"Did the doctor tell you something back there?"

"He didn't have to. I just know. And I'm ready."

I looked away from her. Charlene's house wasn't too far yet, but it grew blurry through my eyes.

Miss Millie touched my shoulder. "Got everything worked out with the preacher man for the particulars of what will happen, when . . ." She smiled at me like she understood I didn't want her to say the word. She picked another one. ". . . when my day comes. But all that stuff considered, this here little guy is the only thing I really worry about once I'm gone."

With that, Clarence looked back at me like he was waiting for me to say something. And looking into his beady eyes, it hit me. "You want me to take care of Clarence for you?"

Clarence seemed to nod as he turned back around as Miss Millie smiled so sweet. "That would make me happy, if it could happen that way. I ran it by your mama and she said it was okay with her. But I understand if it's an imposition."

I wasn't one hundred percent sure what an imposition was, but I knew if Miss Millie would be happy to have me take care of Clarence for her when she . . . was gone, I would do it.

When our walk that day ended, I wasn't surprised to see Miss Millie reach in her pocket. Every now and then she'd still give me another treasure from some part of her life. So far she'd given me old coins, an arrowhead, more rocks, old pins, Ruth's shell and more marbles. I kept them all in that hatbox with the photo.

This time Miss Millie pulled out an envelope. And this envelope had my name on it. Well, to tell the truth, it said, *Alice-girl*.

She put the envelope in my right hand and then cradled my hand with both of hers. She stood there for a moment just looking at me. I was trying to be polite and wait for her to say something, but she didn't so I said, "Thank you."

Then she spoke, her eyes twinkling with tears. "No, Alice-girl, thank *you*."

She hugged me.

I hugged her back, burying my face in her white button-down shirt that smelled of lotion, sunshine and friendship.

Clarence must have felt left out or something, 'cause

he started whining and whimpering like he wanted a hug, too.

Miss Millie laughed. "Don't that beat all?" She picked up Clarence as I started to open the letter. She smiled but said, "No need to open that now. You can open it when ya get home."

"Okay." I laughed, too, as I walked to the fence and hollered back, "See you tomorrow."

. . . . . .

But I was wrong.

chapter **28**

Reverend Hill was in Grandma's living room the next day when I woke up.

When a preacher man is at your house when you wake up, it's probably not because he wants breakfast. So when I saw him in the living room, I suspected it had happened.

When I saw Clarence with him, I knew.

Eddie started crying when Mama explained it to him. I think she was waiting for my tears to come, too, but my insides just felt kind of empty.

. . . . . .

The next three days were out of focus for me.

I know the usual daytime stuff happened, like getting dressed and eating and all. I remember Mama making cookies, Pam trying to get me to laugh and Eddie hugging me lots of times.

But I could barely talk to anyone.

Except Clarence. I knew he was missing her, too.

······

I felt bad leaving Clarence at home for the funeral, but Mama was right, he wouldn't like all the people being there. Not sure I liked everyone being there either.

But I sat there through the whole "ashes to ashes and dust to dust" stuff. Through praying and reading more Bible verses. I sat there, listening.

And then we all walked down to the cemetery for the burial.

That's when Reverend Hill asked if anyone had any last words and Miss Frankie offered to talk, just like Miss Millie said she would.

She held on to a paper fan that looked to have a picture of the Last Supper on it, but it was hard to say for certain, since she fanned herself so fast. "Lordy, it's hot! This home-goin' service is so very hot! That's what we call it. A home-goin' service. Miss Millie's ancestors are all waitin' for her on the other side to welcome her home. Oh how they'll rejoice!" She fanned some more and looked up at the sky.

Everybody waited. Reverend Hill moved closer to her, maybe thinking she was done.

She wasn't.

Finally, she continued. "But she was my very best friend and I'm sure gonna miss her! Can't believe she gone! Gone. Dear Millie! She was a good Christian lady." Miss Frankie stopped for a minute and glared at Miss Mary. She fanned herself some more before continuing. "And *she* was a wonderful singer. And a good baker. Lordy, she was a good baker. She was a good woman and a great friend and I miss her already."

She sighed and lowered her head. Reverend Hill thanked her for her words, but she wasn't quite done yet. "I'll see you one day again, Millie!" Miss Frankie exclaimed, looking up to the sky. And then she added with a twinkle in her eye, "But it won't be soon. You know you *was* a lot older than me . . ."

I just knew Miss Millie would've liked that.

That and all the rest happened just like she said it would.

When the preacher told us he'd like us all to raise our voices to sing Miss Millie's favorite song, Miss Mary had to know it was her last chance to sing a solo that day, so she stood up and cleared her throat. But when Reverend Hill went over and whispered in her ear, I heard her say,

"Humph!" before walking away. I just knew Miss Millie would've liked that, too.

*"Somewhere over the rainbow, skies are blue*
*And the dreams that you dare to dream,*
*Really do come true."*

I didn't really feel like it, but hearing the song reminded me of the day I heard Miss Millie singing so I couldn't help but join in.

And beside me was Mama, who was singing, and signing the song to Eddie, and Pam, who was watching Mama sign like she was trying to soak up how to make every word.

Grandma was standing with us, but not singing, only humming, since I don't think she remembered the words.

When the singing was done, Reverend Hill reminded everyone about the meal back at the church, and folks began to leave the cemetery.

"Mercy me! I almost forgot." Miss Frankie pulled out what looked to be a pie pan and put it on the grave site. "So worried about getting to the repast, I almost forgot to leave this," she told me. "See you at the church hall!"

Did Miss Frankie think Miss Millie was taking pie

orders now? I wanted to laugh but I knew the person who would have laughed the most at that was gone.

All of a sudden, my chest hurt. I felt it rise up and down with such force, like I'd been running. I breathed deep, hoping to make my chest quit panting, and turned to the little cross with the peeling paint next to Miss Millie's grave. I put my hand out like Miss Millie did every time we'd walk this way. I never did know what she was saying, so I hoped Mr. Clayton Miller didn't mind that I didn't have any words.

I'm not sure how long I stood like that but soon I heard Mama call my name to say it was time to go.

I took my hand off the cross and put it inside the pocket of the sundress Mama made me wear. With my hand in my pocket, I felt the family picture Miss Millie gave me that day. Having it inside my pocket made me feel like I had a secret nobody else knew.

I peeked at the picture and just seeing Miss Millie and her family in that happy minute of her life made me as close to happy as I could be right then.

......

Walking into the church's social hall, I was greeted by fried chicken, fried green tomatoes, fried collard greens, you name it and if it could be fried, it was probably laid out on the main table right under the picture of our Lord. I had to smile since it looked like Jesus Himself was offering us the feast as He stood there with His hands stretched out over the food, like He was sayin', *Come and get it!*

I was just finishing some fried chicken I really didn't feel like eating when Miss Frankie came up to me. She grabbed me so hard I would've choked if I hadn't already swallowed my last bite.

"Baby, baby, baby," she said, and rocked me back and forth as if I really was a baby. "What are we gonna do without her? I knew this day would come, but Lordy, Lordy, Lordy, why did it come so soon?"

I wasn't sure if she was asking that question to me or to the Lord, but it didn't really matter since I couldn't answer. I could hardly even breathe.

When she finally released me, I caught my breath and asked her, "Did you put a *pie pan* on Miss Millie's grave?"

"Mmm-hmmm." Miss Frankie nodded and smiled like she was remembering those pies.

"Can you tell me why?"

She nodded again. "It's an old tradition of ours. We put something that belonged to the deceased on their grave to help them have a good journey to where they goin'. Figured the pie pan is as good as anything, since I had it at my house. And that way, when I meet her again she can't be claimin' I never returned it!" Miss Frankie let out a laugh, but I saw real tears in her eyes. She looked at me and smoothed back a piece of my hair that came out of its pigtail. "Plus, it helps us say our goodbyes."

My words got all stuck in my throat as I tried to take this all in, so I just moved my head up and down.

Someone came up to hug Miss Frankie, and I wandered off. The huge table of food was completely picked over, except for a mystery vegetable casserole, so people started to leave.

There were chores to be done, just like every other day.

There were jobs to be worked, just like every other day.

But my job of walking with Miss Millie wouldn't happen again like every other day. I was starting to feel the pain of the loss of it and of her, just like when I had to leave behind my home and friends in Ohio.

Mama saw me sitting by myself under the blue stained-glass window and came over. "You okay, Alice-Ann?"

And even though my heart felt like it was made out of lead right then, I was remembering what Miss Millie said about figuring out what you can change and what you can't change. I figured nobody but Jesus could bring somebody back from the dead, so I needed to go ahead and finish getting sad, and finish getting mad. It was like Miss Millie was whispering in my ear right then and there, telling me it was time to get smart and figure out what to do next. I tried to smile as I answered, "I think I'll be okay, Mama."

Then I looked back at that picture of the Lord with His hands stretched out, and I pictured Him getting ready to welcome Miss Millie to be forever with her Clayton, both her Jameses and her friend Miss Ruth, all together in one perfect place.

And then I did smile. But only for a second because I felt like there was still something I needed to do.

I thought of Miss Frankie leaving Miss Millie a pie pan. If there was one dang thing I could do to help Miss Millie on her last journey, I had to do it now.

After all, she'd helped me so much on mine.

chapter **29**

I knew just what I needed.

The hatbox.

The hatbox filled with all the treasures from Miss Millie. One of them might help Miss Millie on her journey. And if Miss Frankie was right, leaving her something just might help me say goodbye, too. Although that was hard to imagine.

But I had to at least try.

Running upstairs to the bed I shared with Mama, I lifted up the corner of the gold bedspread, expecting to see the box sitting under the bed where I always kept it. But it wasn't there.

I bent down on all fours and shoved my head way

back under the rusty springs that creaked every time one of us rolled over in the middle of the night.

But I saw nothing.

A piece of my pigtail got stuck on the spring under the bed and I had to wiggle and twist it loose before I could jump up and check out the closet.

But again, nothing.

. . . . . .

Then of course I thought of Eddie.

Every time I came home with something new, he would hold it and smile and play with it till I made him put it back.

He loved that box almost as much as I loved it.

He had to have it!

I found Eddie in the backyard and signed, "Do you know where my hatbox is?"

Eddie looked away, playing a game he sometimes played, like you can't be holding him responsible for something if he can't see you ask.

I knew better.

"Eddie," I signed as I stepped back in front of him, knowing he knew. "Where is it? It's mine and I need it. Now!"

Eddie sighed, grinned real big, shrugged his shoulders and signed, "Get on bus."

I'd had enough. "No, Eddie, I don't want to play! Tell me where my box is."

Eddie grinned. "Get on bus and I show you," he signed.

Mama always talks about her blood boiling when she gets real mad. I don't know at what temperature that happens, but I was fairly certain my blood was at the temperature for boiling right then.

But knowing Eddie like I did, and figuring I had no choice, I took a deep breath and got in line behind my brother as he drove that crazy plate around the backyard like we were on a bus.

The more we crisscrossed the yard, the madder I got.

Just when my blood was ready to completely boil over and I was about to jump off that bus and tell Mama, Eddie stopped "driving" and pointed to a hollowed-out spot behind the big tree with the tire swing. Right there at the bottom was a little indent, the perfect size for hiding a box of treasures.

And there it was.

And right beside it was Clarence like he was guarding it for me until I could do what he knew I needed to do.

I signed to Eddie, "Why did you take it?"

Eddie moved his hand across his forehead like he was wiping away a memory—the sign for *forget*—and then he shook his head something fierce.

"I don't want to forget," he repeated.

I answered by touching my heart and his. "Don't worry. You won't forget. I promise. We'll never forget. We'll keep everything in here and we'll always remember."

Clarence snuggled close to us and nudged us to pet him and the three of us shared a hug.

For a few minutes I just sat there with Eddie and Clarence, next to the hatbox, and I knew we were all three remembering Miss Millie.

Mama came out and sat down next to us on that bit of grass, under that tree. "You guys okay out here?"

Eddie nodded, wiped his eyes and went back to plate-driving while I rubbed the hatbox like I was petting Clarence. "I think so. But there's still something I have to do. For Miss Millie."

Mama looked at me and at the hatbox, her eyes getting misty again. I looked down at the box to keep my eyes from doing the same. I read aloud the words on the hatbox. "'*Moveo et proficio.*' Do you know what that means, Mama?"

Mama looked at the box and then up at the sky. "Hmmm . . . Let me think—I studied Latin years ago. Wait—I should know this. Oh, I remember: '*Moveo et proficio*' is Latin for 'I move and I progress.'"

Didn't that beat all? "Did you just make that up right now?"

Mama laughed. A real kind of laugh that made me feel more at home than I had felt for a long time. "I promise—that's what it means."

I hugged Mama and told her I had to go do that last thing for Miss Millie. Mama asked if I wanted her to come, but I told her no—I could do this by myself.

Well—by myself with Clarence.

I grabbed the hatbox and Clarence and headed out to the front yard, where I ran smack into Jake and Pam.

Pam just walked on around to the backyard to find Eddie, but Jake stopped in front of me. "Hey."

I wasn't in a mood to chat, but knowing I was heading to where Miss Millie was, it was like she was nudging me to be nice. "Hey," I managed to say back.

He nodded to Clarence. "Y'all takin' care of him now?"

"Uh-huh," I said, bobbing my head up and down.

Jake leaned over to pet Clarence, who must've remembered him saving his life and all, 'cause his tail started wagging real happy-like. Jake laughed as he pet-ted him some more.

I just stood there, wanting to go, when Jake stopped petting him and looked me right in the eye. "She was real nice, wasn't she?"

I nodded again.

And still looking right in my eyes, Jake McHale said the darndest thing. "Can I come over sometime? Maybe with Pam? Ya know, to see the dog and all?"

And since the boy plumb saved the dog's life, I couldn't very well tell him no, could I? "Sure." I nodded again.

Jake beamed and stood up. "Thanks!" And then he saw Eddie and Pam walking out front. Pam motioned for Eddie to look at Jake, whose face turned all serious-like, like he was getting ready to perform a speech he'd been practicing.

"Go ahead—like I taught ya," Pam encouraged her brother.

Jake then signed in a kind of awkward way, "Hi, Eddie." By the time he got done fingerspelling Eddie's name, I wasn't sure which one of those boys had the big-ger smile on their face.

Maybe Pam's smile was biggest of all.

But my own heart wasn't ready to smile just yet. I had to get back to Miss Millie.

chapter **30**

Clarence and I made it to the cemetery in pretty good time. Somehow, with Miss Millie gone, Clarence didn't mind me walking him at all anymore.

But when we got to that old, rusty iron gate, I just couldn't go on in. My feet froze to the dry and dusty ground. It wasn't because I was scared this time.

I knew I needed to get to Miss Millie. But more than that, I knew deep in my heart that when I left her this time, it really would be the last time.

She was gone.

Miss Millie was gone.

I sat down in the dirt right there, outside the cemetery.

While I was hugging both the hatbox and Clarence tight to my chest, my tears . . . the same tears that had been stuck inside for the last few days . . . finally decided to fall. Clarence let himself be held like that, even rubbing his head against mine, like he was offering himself as a hankie.

And I cried and cried some more.

Not sure how long we sat like that, but all at once, through my tears, right there at the gate of the cemetery, I heard something behind us. I gasped, making Clarence jump back and growl. My hurt heart started thudding out of fear.

Then I saw what was making the noise.

Right there, like they all knew I didn't really want to be alone, stood Eddie, Pam and Jake.

"What are you guys doing here?" I asked, sniffing, wiping my eyes on the back of my arm.

Pam spoke first. "We . . . um . . . we know how y'all hate cemeteries and we had a feeling y'all was headed here." Then she grinned at me.

I stood up, brushed off my sundress and smiled back. "Thanks." I looked at each of them standing there. My voice was shaking like I was back on Grandma's bumpy road. "Maybe I'm starting to not mind cemeteries so much, now. But I'm glad you guys are here."

Eddie grinned and signed, "Never forget." I nodded

and turned to walk through the wrought-iron gate of the cemetery as everyone followed.

Together, we walked way to the back of the cemetery, past the bench under the old oak tree, past the big gravestones and past all the pretty flowers until I found the grave site of Miss Millie. The workers had just covered up the grave, so the Georgia clay was glistening red and shiny in the sunshine. Mama promised we would buy her a cross to match Mr. Clayton's.

I first headed back over to Mr. Clayton's cross and put my hand on it again. Eddie, Pam and Jake stood back, giving Clarence and me some privacy, like I used to do for Miss Millie. Unlike earlier, this time I found some words. "Mr. Clayton, I'm happy you and Miss Millie are back together. But I'm sorry she had to leave here to make that happen. And I wish your boy could be with you in this place—but I know you're all together where it really counts."

Then I looked at Clarence, who I swear was looking right at me, listening. "Please take care of Miss Millie for us, okay?"

Clarence's tooth stuck out even more, like he was telling me that was exactly what he wanted to say.

And then I turned to the shining mound of clay

showing me where Miss Millie was buried. I just stood there for a few minutes not saying anything, but hoping my heart said something I couldn't.

Finally, I knelt on the hard Georgia ground. Clarence turned around in a circle like he was trying to figure out how to kneel, but instead finally sat down next to me.

And sitting right there in the back of the cemetery, a panting dog at my side, with an audience I never would've expected so close by, I thought about my time in Rainbow.

I thought of Daddy and how a small part of me would always be waiting for him, even though he might never show up.

I thought of Mama and how a big part of me would always be glad she made me go see Miss Millie that one day.

And I thought of Miss Millie and me and how different we were. But what made us different wasn't one lick as important as what made us the same. Me and Miss Millie knew that.

Then I pulled out the hatbox full of all the treasures she'd shared with me. If a pie plate might help Miss Millie on her journey, one of these treasures surely couldn't hurt. I looked through the box.

It was funny—when she gave them to me, they were just things. But now they were so much more. I wasn't sure I could part with any of them.

But then I saw it.

Miss Ruth's scallop shell.

*We might all come from different directions,* she'd said. *But hopefully, we all end up at the same place one day.* I pulled it out and wrapped my fingers around it like that day Miss Millie gave it to me. And then I put it in the spot close to where her cross would go.

Then there was one more thing I had to give her. I pulled out a folded piece of paper from my pocket and recited the poem I wrote for her.

*I'm happy you're in heaven.*
*It's where you deserve to be.*
*But still I know each step I take*
*You'll always walk with me.*

I don't know if it was as good as Daddy's poems, but I liked it just fine and I bet Miss Millie would have, too. Writing her a poem felt kind of like talking to her—it made me feel better. I folded the poem back up and put it under Miss Ruth's shell.

Picking up the hatbox again, I saw my letter. I'd read it so many times I had it memorized. But I needed to read it again.

*Alice-girl,*

> *I never been one to get all mushy so no need to start now.*
> *But I want to make sure you know you're a real fine young lady.*
> *You said there's no rainbows in Rainbow.*
> *But I disagree. You're a rainbow in a sometimes dark world.*
> *Keep shining, my Alice-girl. Keep shining.*
>
> *Love,*
> *Mrs. Millie Miller*

I looked again at that old hatbox, thinking about those Latin words, and started to think, for a hatbox, it was pretty smart. Maybe sometimes you do have to move to progress—and end up where you're supposed to be.

But speaking of moving and progressing, I knew for a dang fact that Miss Millie would not want any of us sitting there getting all mushy in that cemetery on her account for much longer.

I picked up my hatbox of treasures and started walking back to my friends.

But before I walked away from Miss Millie's resting place, I looked up to heaven.

On this clear summer day, there was not a cloud in the sky.

But I swear that there, high in the sky, shining like nobody's business, was the prettiest rainbow I ever did see.

I smiled as I heard Miss Millie's voice saying, "Don't that beat all!"

And it did! Miss Millie and that rainbow sure did.

# ACKNOWLEDGMENTS

I thank every author of every book used in a book report I graded as an English teacher, prompting me to want to write novels, too.

To my agent Steven Chudney, for believing in my first manuscript when it still had far to go and for pushing me to go deeper to make it better and better, I am so grateful. And for managing to get the amazing Nancy Paulsen on board as editor, I am beyond thankful. Nancy's brilliant insights into my make-believe world made me fall in love with these characters like they were family. And her love for them made me trust the editing process like I never had before. Nancy's awesome assistant, Sara LaFleur, and everyone who worked on this impressed me with their incredible care, kindness, and craft.

The writing process could become a lonely art form. But with people like my writing "twin," Laura Smith, who offer encouragement, prayers, critiques, and friendship, it is absolutely a blessing.

Every early reader offered insights and inspiration that proved immensely helpful. Thank you all for giving me your time, opinions, and support.

And I wouldn't want to write without the love and support of my family:

My mom and dad, who first told me I could write and never stopped believing it.

My sister, Kathy, whose love of books inspired me.

My brother, Tim, whose world of silence gave me fruitful ground on which to grow Alice's brother's world.

To Megan, Katey, Ryan, and Evan, nothing I will ever do in life will be as wonderful and meaningful as being your mom. Thank you for being.

And to Brad: for more than thirty years, you have given me support, praise, (constructive) criticism, encouragement, and, of course, your love. "Thank you" doesn't seem like enough.

To all my students at Colerain High School (and every student in the world), the book you are holding in your hands right now was once just a dream. Your dreams are just as possible—don't let anyone tell you differently.

Finally, thank you to Miss Martha, whose daily dog-walks with my young daughter planted a tiny seed.